THE HOUSE WITHOUT WINDOWS

BY

BARBARA NEWHALL F

Illustrated.

NEW YORK:
ALFRED A. KNOPF, INC,
1927.

'LIL BEETHOVEN PUBLISHERS
NEW YORK, NEW YORK
ROCKEFELLER CENTER

Contents

CHAPTER I

THE MEADOW

Flowers have faded,
Butterfly wings are weary,
And far off is the chanting
of the eternal sea.

In a little brown shingled cottage on one of the foothills of Mount Varcrobis, there lived with her father and mother, Mr. and Mrs. Eigleen, a little girl named Eepersip. She was rather lonely.

She kept advising Mr. and Mrs. Eigleen to make a beautiful garden, where flowers would bloom year after year, and to which birds and butterflies would come back again and again. Accordingly all three set to work with a will, and in a few years they had made the most beautiful garden that was ever seen. Around its borders bloomed apple-trees, pear-trees, and peach-trees, and inside them bloomed azaleas, rhododendrons, magnolias, lilacs, honeysuckle, and fire-blossoms. Next came the ground flowers. There were seven kinds of roses, and there was a whole corner devoted to early spring flowers: crocuses, daffodils, squills, and narcissi. Another corner was carpeted with tender anemones, all snow-white. In the center of the garden there was a circular bed filled with iris of all kinds and colors. Clematis and morning-glory vines climbed over the wooden benches, and near the center was a tall arch with ramblers climbing all over it. Another bed was thickly clustered with great purple violets. The paths through the garden had gracefully bending ferns on each side.

For the first few months Eepersip was delighted with her flowers, and the butterflies and birds pleased her even more. But she was not a child who could be contented easily, and pretty soon she began to feel lonely again. One July day a fresh idea came into her head. She packed some sandwiches and some crackers in a small lunch-basket. Without telling a soul, the next morning before dawn she slipped out of bed, dressed, and picked up her basket; then stole out of the cottage and away. She went east from her home on a shady path through beautiful woodlands, with here and there a grove of great massive pines.

And as she walked she sang merrily.

After quite a while she stepped out of the woodlands on to a large lawn. Close to the path there was a pool with some tiny goldfishes swimming about in it. Then she knew that she was nearing a house, and instead of pacing slowly along the path she began to run; for she was afraid that someone would see her and send her back home. But after a few minutes she grew tired and settled down to a reasonable pace. And as she slowed down she came into an enormous field of rhododendrons, lavender, white, and brilliant red. Oh, what a gorgeous place that was! As Eepersip walked along, an oriole sang from a bush; she peeped into a humming-bird's nest with two tiny white eggs in it; she startled a vireo from its nest in a law clump of grass, and, peeping into it, found three baby birds. The farther she went the more her heart began to leap within her for joy of the life she was finding for herself. Her loneliness decreased, and she was as free and happy as the birds or butterflies.

Soon the red and lavender rhododendrons dropped out, leaving only the white; then the white ones too lessened in thickness until there were none left. All this while she had been slowly climbing Mount Varcrobis itself. At last she came into a small open glade, still walking east from the cottage – which she was not thinking about just then, so happy was she at thought of the new, interesting life she had found. This glade was near the top of the mountain, only one high peak towering above it. Across it ran a little brook, tinkling through the ferns and bracken.

She paused on the path suddenly, then drew back; for a doe and her daisied fawn were grazing close by. Eepersip took from her basket a lump of sugar, and held it out to the beautiful creatures. Very hesitatingly the doe moved forward, followed by her fawn, and at last took the lump of sugar from Eepersip's fingers.

Eepersip had not expected this. On the contrary, she had thought that they would be startled and would bound away out of sight in the woods. She gazed silently at the doe, who had begun to graze again without a sign of fear. Could it be a dream? she thought. Eepersip had experienced the delightful sensation of the doe's slightly rough tongue around her fingers; and suddenly she felt as if she could never leave them – as if she must stay always and play with the woods. Already she had become acquainted with a doe and a fawn, and they were not afraid of her! She sat down on the grass, and the fawn lay beside her. She cuddled it close in her arms.

Then it grew dark. The sun was sinking, and at last it went behind a thin, filmy cloud, producing wonderful colors, red, gold, silver, and purple. Like fire it glowed and quivered, and through it all could be seen the ball of the sun, growing clearer as it sank, and growing larger too. And as Eepersip sprang to her feet and watched it glow and quiver, she saw, away off, an enormous range of mountains; and where the mountains left off there was the edge of the ocean, with the light of the dying day reflected in it, in purples, reds, and yellows.

And then, being very tired, she lay down on the grass beside the two deer; and in a few seconds she was sound asleep.

*****

The next morning Eepersip was surprised to find herself lying there on the grass between the doe and her fawn; she had forgotten about running away. The first thing she thought of was her breakfast; for, not having had anything to eat the day before except a few handfuls of delicious red berries which she had found growing on a thick vine, she was very hungry. Not a sandwich in her basket had she touched; she had been so fascinated with her adventure that she had not thought of them. But now she ate three whole ones, ever and again breaking off bits and feeding them to the deer.

When she had finished, she set off in a great hurry to explore her surroundings. First she walked down in the direction of the beautiful sunset she had seen, a little off the direction of the path by which she had ascended, and came to a great rocky precipice, the side of the mountain. She looked down and far off she saw a shining river winding about in the valley below, sometimes twisting back upon itself, then straightening out again. But it made her giddy to look too long, and she turned and started back to where she had slept. The doe and her fawn were grazing quietly when Eepersip returned. She threw herself on her back and gazed at the clear blue sky. In it swallows with their snowy breasts were circling, and when the sun shone full on them their white wings glimmered like the ice on a winter's day. A great desire came over Eepersip. She wanted to fly and swoop through the air like the swallows. She thought to herself that they had always been her favorite birds. She had always marveled at their flight, as now they twisted in giant corkscrews and now swerved so as to turn almost completely over.

A butterfly flew over her head – a little yellow butterfly who danced and glimmered before her.

Her brown eyes sparkled with delight. A cricket hopped and twittered; a bird burst into song. Almost without knowing what she did Eepersip leaped into the air and began to dance, with the swallows circling above her head and the leaves fluttering about her. Then suddenly she sat down, breathless. She began stripping off her shoes and stockings. Her feet were tender, and every stick she stepped on hurt; but she was determined to get her feet toughened so as to go barefoot all the time.

Now, directly east of this fairy glade there was a steep slope which ascended to the very summit of Mount Varcrobis, called Eiki-ennern Peak. Eepersip had a fascinated eye for this slope and longed to see what was at the top of it, but she would not leave the deer just yet, and also she was determined not to put on her shoes and stockings again. So she decided to stay in the soft grass until her feet were toughened; and she thought that then she could go up that wonderful peak over which the sun rose in clouds of glory every morning.

Before Eepersip had danced long she walked down toward the great precipice again, with her shoes and stockings under her arms. The instant she got there a madness came upon her, and *whizz!* Two shoes and two stockings were flying through the air at a tremendous rate. They landed in the trees far below, while Eepersip, glad to get rid of them, coolly returned to the glade, thinking that her feet were already tougher than before because of that bold act. When she got back she decided to rest a while, then walk in the opposite direction and see what was at the northern end of the glade. So when she got rested she started off that way, with the doe and the fawn trotting beside her. At last she came to the slope of the mountain on that side. But this, instead of being a sheer precipice; was a gradually falling grassy bank, down which they went. The doe and the fawn followed some distance; then they turned back, letting Eepersip go on alone. But when she got part way to the bottom she began to see houses; and so, deciding that that wasn't the side for her, she ran back as fast as she could.

*****

Meanwhile Mr. and Mrs. Eigleen were wondering in vain where their poor child had gone. At first they hadn't thought much about her, for she had been lost in the woods several times before and had always found her way home safely. But when it came to being gone two or three days, why, they were not sure that they were awake! The child must be starving, and who knew what a tender morsel to some prowling animal she might be by this time? So they began to grieve greatly over their loss, for they dearly loved Eepersip.

Before they had missed her very long, a poor old woman and her husband had climbed that part of Mount Varcrobis. Nobody in the village down below cared much for Mr. and Mrs. Ikkisfield, as they were called; and they had decided to go elsewhere and see if they could find some friends. The Eigleens took pity on them, and at last persuaded them to live in the brown cottage in the woods, and to let the Eigleens themselves go to the house of friends of theirs, the Wraspanes. It was the Wraspanes' rhododendron field that Eepersip had thought so beautiful.

The Eigleens, being exceedingly kind people, gladly gave up their cottage and their beautiful garden to Mr. and Mrs. Ikkisfield. Indeed, these things were no joy to them, now that they had lost Eepersip, for whose sake they had made the garden. The old couple were delighted, and, thanking the Eigleens very kindly, they moved in that same evening, the Eigleens leaving some of their belongings with them.

Eepersip stayed for many days with the doe and her fawn, and then, her feet having become tough, she crossed the brooklet and went on up Eiki-ennern Peak. Near the top, in a small sheltered place, she found a dear little pool surrounded with moss and ferns, amongst which some iris bloomed. It had a sandy bottom, over which swam tiny silver minnows. When they turned over and the sun shone on their bellies Eepersip saw a streak of silver. At last, when she got to the top, she saw that on one side it was a vast daisied slope, down, down; and on another it was wooded to the foot. From where she stood, range after range spread out before her, lake after lake beneath her, with the crimson of the now setting sun gloriously reflected in them. It was like fairyland. And when Eepersip turned southward, she beheld the almighty ocean, with the exquisite sunset colors reflected in it as in the lakes. That night she slept on a soft bed of moss in a hollow down near the pool.

The next morning, after she had made a good breakfast on the juicy root of a plant which she found, she lay down by the pool and gazed at the sky, the way she had done on the second day of her wildness. And as she lay there it grew so quiet that a chipmunk stole out of a tiny hole that he had dug between the roots of a tree. He came to her, sniffed at a cracker she was munching, and tickled her cheek with his nose; whereupon she cautiously put out her hand with a piece of the cracker on it. The chipmunk was frightened and ran away. But the piece of cracker looked very tempting, and before long he lost his fear and ventured close again. Step by step he crept along, until, with a frightened squeal, he seized the piece and disappeared. Eepersip waited, laughing. In a few minutes he came back again, and this time he took the piece that she held out to him, running only a few steps. The third time he took it calmly and deliberately and ate it without running at all, evidently convinced that Eepersip was a friend. And the fourth time he was even more bold, going so far as to sit on her stomach while he ate. But by that time, between them, they had licked the platter clean – the cracker was gone.

"Just like the doe and her fawn," Eepersip thought. How fearless he was, the fuzzy brown little creature! It seemed to happy Eepersip that all the wild was ready to make friends, as if nothing were afraid of her. She felt more than ever that she could never leave these entrancing forests. She could never, never go back, she mused. How wonderful it was to lie there watching the things that were happening, and actually to have one of the inhabitants of these woods – a timid one that was usually afraid – come up to her and eat from her hand! This adventure had certainly tightened in her heart the desire to stay always and become acquainted with more and more creatures – with the swallows she loved so well, and with the little fairy butterflies.

Whenever she went down to the sheltered spot by the pool, she saw so many beautiful things here and there that she never knew what to do in her delight. Iris blossomed in gold and blue; butterflies danced overhead like yellow rose-petals flying in the breeze. Once, running over to the pool, she found a tiny beach, about fifteen inches long and half a foot wide – no more than a handful of sand completely hidden in a forest of ferns. Across it ran the chipmunk's footprints, and the marks of his wee claws could be plainly seen in the damp sand. That little beach was the earth's dear treasure, so it seemed to Eepersip, alone in that wild place. In the fields all around, thousands of buttercups blossomed, and great beds of daisies whitened the earth's brown surface.

In one place, among dark ferns, grew columbine, gay little gypsies curtseying in the breeze. Their colors spoke to her of dawn, gold sunset and white clouds, snow-banks fringed with icicles, night sky entwined with moonbeams, black clouds and radiant sun, or orange, yellow, and scarlet leaves – autumn leaves. She gathered some, and made a rainbow wreath of blossoms; and curling about her hair, they danced again.

Beneath the branches of a white pine grew blushing lady-slippers, which Eepersip had never seen before. "Dawn comes to earth sometimes," she thought, "bringing her flower-clouds and clasping them with pearl seeds."

Eepersip was anxious to know what was on the southern slope of this highest peak of Mt.

Varcrobis. So one day along she went, happily singing, until she came to it. Then she was surprised to find that this slope, instead of being a rocky precipice as the one had been at the foot of Eiki-ennern Peak, went down steeply for a little way and then broadened out into an enormous field, on the farther side of which was a herd of deer.

Away, away, Eepersip could just see to the edge of this plain-like field. With a shout, down she dashed; and, dancing as she had never danced before, she sang like a nightingale for joy of her discovery. And yet, she thought to herself, what if it should be a dream? She was quite sure that it was not, though, for she had felt decidedly awake when she started off. But, because she had started before anyone else was up or even awake, she thought that she might be asleep herself. Anyhow, if it was a dream, it was a lovely one, and she need not worry.

*****

But now let us return to the grieving parents of Eepersip, who were consulting the Wraspanes about a plan to search for her.

At last Mrs. Eigleen said: "Something very queer has happened to our child. She must have seen something or other that has made her want to go off. But I will tell you what we can do. We'll take the Wraspanes' big tent, and, fetching the Ikkis-fields, we can camp near where one of us sees Eepersip; for I'm sure that she wouldn't leave Mount Varcrobis unless absolutely compelled to. We can learn what habits Eepersip has got into, and perhaps we can catch her by some plan. My husband and you, Mr. Wraspane, are the spry ones, and perhaps you can hide behind trees and catch her when she goes past." "What a grand idea!" cried everybody else in one voice; and without further ado they decided to carry it out.

So the very next day Mr. Eigleen and Mr. Wraspane set off to explore, on the chance of finding Eepersip or discovering where she was living. They reasoned out that Eepersip must have gone through the Wraspanes' land when running off; because on the western side of the Eigleens' little cottage there was a dense wood, of which Eepersip had always been rather afraid, it was so dark and mysterious. They went through the field of rhododendrons, on the selfsame path, and at last came out in the same small glade in which Eepersip had seen the deer, with the same brooklet running across it. They hunted all over it, but no trace of Eepersip could they find. They began to feel foolish. They decided to go back and tell the waiting folks that they had not seen a glimpse of her, when a glorious burst of singing reached their ears. Immediately they turned and ran in the direction of the voice. But still they didn't see her, for they never dreamed that she had gone up the steep slope of Eiki-ennern Peak. And they began to feel still more foolish.

At last, after a lot of aimless wandering through forests, glades, and fields, they decided to give it up for just then and tell the folks that they had heard her but couldn't find her. So back they went, feeling very foolish indeed.

"We were looking for her everywhere," said Mr. Eigleen, "and after we had searched for a long time we heard this excellent singing, better than I thought she could utter, and we went in its direction but couldn't find her. So I am beginning to think that 'twasn't she at all – either she or a fairy."

"Fairy!" exclaimed Mrs. Eigleen, indignantly – "fairy! There is no such thing as 'fairy' – stupid!" Mr. Eigleen cast a wink at his partner hunter, Mr. Wraspane. "Anyhow," said he, "fairy or none, we heard the singing."

Again Mrs. Eigleen burst out with: "But why didn't you go right *to* the sound?"

"Dear wife," said Mr. Eigleen, "we couldn't, because directly in front of that sound there was a very steep rocky slope – you know very well the slope of Eiki-ennern Peak."

"Well," said Mrs. Eigleen, "if the voice came from behind that slope, Eepersip must have got to the top of Eiki-ennern Peak somehow, and if *she* did, *you* can. Wait with us a while and have lunch, and then go and try to find her again, and I will come with you."

"All right," said Mr. Eigleen.

Accordingly, after lunch all three started off on a fresh quest. They searched the little glade high, and low once more, but with the same ill luck. Really Eepersip saw them all the time, but while they were here she was there, and while they were there she was here, all the time keeping out of sight behind bushes and trees. And when she rustled the leaves and they heard her, they thought that it was just the breezes making commotion in the leaves and grass.

Before they had hunted very long Mrs. Eigleen had to admit that the new game was harder than it looked; yet she didn't give it up, for her greatest hope was to have Eepersip back again. At length Eepersip lost sight of them and, thinking that they had gone, she began to sing. They all started, and began to run in the direction of the voice. This time they didn't hesitate to go right up the steep slope of Eiki-ennern Peak. Mrs. Eigleen leading, they all three dashed up, with not a thought of the brambles that they were getting into.

When they got to the top, what a sight met their puzzled eyes! There was Eepersip dancing to her own singing, and ever and again she looked up at a little butterfly which fluttered over her head, and curtseyed before it. Great waves of happiness were flowing through her all the time. They made no effort to call her, but only stood enchanted until she danced off to the field. Then they quickly walked away.

First they went back to their own little cottage and collected some of the important belongings which they had left there. Next they went on to the Wraspanes' house and got the tent and other necessary things.

Then, with the Ikkisfields and the Wraspanes, they started off for the top of Eiki-ennern Peak.

They pitched the tent rather far from the pool, but very near where they had seen Eepersip, on top of the hill. Now the next problem was to make the plans; and as soon as the tent was up they gathered together and began to think up ways and means. But Mr. Eigleen said: "Let us go on an exploration and discover some of Eepersip's habits. Let us all wander around a while, and when we discover what sort of habits Eepersip has got into, we can make our plans accordingly; for we can't make plans until we *do* know some of her habits."

All approved of what he had said, and everybody prepared himself for a long walk, interrupted at times by hiding and lurking, peeping and sneaking. So each person had a bite to eat and set off to explore the surroundings. They hunted high and low, but never saw a sign of Eepersip – never had a chance to peep and sneak. That evening, however, while they were talking things over, they heard another burst of singing. They leaped to their feet and, taking a big lantern, all started out of the tent. In the direction of the singing they went on, trying to walk rather fast, but also trying not to step on many leaves or dry twigs so as to make a noise; and when they talked it was in the softest whisper. The singing sounded nearer and nearer; but they could not see very well without the lantern (which they didn't light yet for fear of frightening Eepersip away); it was darkening rapidly, and things were very dim. At last the singing grew so loud and so near that they felt almost as if they were about to run into it. And so they actually did; for Eepersip, who had all the time been approaching them as they approached her, went right between the Ikkisfields, startling them so that they didn't know what to do! Mr. Ikkisfield managed to put out his hand and grab her dress, calling for someone to come and help him hold her. But by this time Eepersip had discarded her real dress and had woven one of ferns for herself; and, the ferns being interlaced rather loosely, the one Mr. Ikkisfield caught hold of tore away. Quick as a flash Eepersip bounded away into the night. Thus their first chance of catching her slipped between their fingers. They went back to the tent rather discouraged.

*****

Now the deer in the great field knew Eepersip, and they all loved her, because she was so kind to them. Even the little fawns loved her and made no attempt to run away when she appeared. Twilight and dawn, when the deer were all lying down, were her favorite times in the field. Then she would dance about in her fern dress, singing so sweetly that all the birds watched her. She began to love the birds and butterflies even more than in the first days of her wildness, and almost worshipped them.

The morning after this curious face-to-face meeting with Eepersip, Mr. Eigleen spoke about another plan. "Eepersip every morning comes up from wherever she sleeps to get a drink of water from the little pool. Now do you know that big pine-tree that stands beside the pool?"

"Yes," said Mrs. Eigleen.

"Well, I will go and hide behind that tree to-morrow morning, and when she comes up to the pool I will try to catch her by jumping out at her when she comes by."

"Why do you not do it this morning?" inquired Mrs. Ikkisfield.

"Well, you see," replied Mr. Eigleen, "she has had her morning drink, for I saw her as I was getting out of bed."

"I see," said Mrs. Ikkisfield. "But be sure that you get up in time next morning."

"I will," said Mr. Eigleen. "But if you're up and awake before I am, be sure to pull me by my left ear."

Eepersip was becoming more wary, now she had discovered that they were trying to catch her.

But still she took it as a sort of joke. In the first place, she thought she could easily escape again if they did catch her. But she very much doubted if they could do it. For hours every day she practiced running, leaping, dancing, and prowling, until she was as fleet as a deer and as soft on her feet as a lynx. She had practiced leaping over high objects, and if someone were chasing her she could now escape being cornered by jumping a fence. She had trained herself until, even without a running start, she could clear the back of a standing fawn; or, with a start, a large buck standing full height. All these exercises made her light as a feather and graceful as a fern.

The next morning when Mr. Eigleen woke up, there was hardly a ray of light, but dawn was breaking out here and there. Mr. Eigleen got all ready for an exciting morning. Without waking anybody, he seated himself out in front of the tent, on the side next the field, in such a position that he could see Eepersip when she came up, and where he could pull-to the front flap immediately and bolt out the back way to the tree by the pool without her seeing him. He waited a few minutes, and then he saw her head bobbing up the bank. Hurriedly he closed the front flap before she saw him. Slipping out the other end and round in a long curve, he ran at full speed to the pool and hid behind the big pine.

Now it was at the foot of the pine that Eepersip usually stooped over to drink, because there the water was deeper and clearer. When Eepersip came up the bank, she stared curiously at the tent, thinking: "What! Are my parents still here?" Then on she went to the pool. She approached it in a roundabout direction, her face drawn with suspicion but, as usual, her route ended at the gnarled roots of the big pine– no instinct could draw her away from it.

Mr. Eigleen stirred the leaves gently as she bent over. She lay down flat by the tree, cupped her hands, and began to drink. Very quietly Mr. Eigleen put his hands on her, one on either shoulder, knowing that her dress of ferns would tear. She started, and struggled so violently that his hands relaxed their grip on her shoulders, sliding down her arms, so that they were now hand in hand. That was all Eepersip needed. With a tremendous sweep she took her feet off the ground, dragging down on his arms with all her weight and strength. Mr. Eigleen couldn't relax either of his hands, for she now held them fast. With another sweep she put her feet up on his shoulders and over his head; then, wrenching her own hands free, she slid down his back and slipped away before he could seize her.

When Mr. Eigleen went home everyone was surprised at this acrobatic adventure.

Mrs. Eigleen made a plan now. "Sometime at midnight," she said, "we could take a covered lantern and go down on the meadow to try to find out where Eepersip sleeps. I know the meadow is very large, but common sense tells me that she would sleep near the woods; so, tomorrow night let's go and try to find her."

"Er-er-I don't know," replied Mr. Eigleen. "I'm a little bit afraid of that meadow, such curious things are happening there all the time."

"What has happened yet?" snapped Mrs. Eigleen. "You're an old coward, you are. I'd go in a minute to save Eepersip."

"So'd I, so'd I,", said Mr. Eigleen, hurriedly. "I only think that there is some curious magic about that field."

"I agree with you there," said Mrs. Eigleen. "But, as I said before, when it comes to saving Eepersip I'd go into thicker magic than there is in the field."

So they planned to get up a little after midnight and circle the field near the edge of the woods; and as there were six of them, Eepersip wouldn't have much chance of

14

escaping if they once got their hands on her. That evening they ate a light supper and went to bed early, and about one o'clock they got up and went out into the great field with a hooded lantern. They circled around it; and at last they found Eepersip hidden in the bushes on the farther edge. Very gently all six laid hands upon her at once.

"Ah, we've captured her!" they cried triumphantly. "Our labors have been rewarded!"

But Eepersip, finding herself caught, became angry, and cried in a loud, commanding voice: "Put me down! Drop me immediately!" She added quietly to herself: "Now it's all over."

Then she began to struggle very violently indeed. They had hold of her securely, and so her struggles were in vain. But just as they carried her past a sleeping doe which had no fawn, she uttered a shrill, wild cry; and this so startled the six that they almost dropped her. The doe woke up; and though she was afraid for herself, she was more afraid for Eepersip. She came galloping after them.

To see the doe galloping swiftly toward them naturally startled old Mrs. Ikkisfield, who supposed that wild animals would flee at the sight of a human being. That was so generally – but not when Eepersip was in danger! Now, Mrs. Ikkisfield had hold of the most important part of Eepersip's anatomy, though no one suspected it at the time – namely, her feet. Mrs. Ikkisfield dropped them, and for the fraction of an instant which Eepersip needed they were allowed to touch the ground. Eepersip wrenched herself free and leaped to the back of the trembling, excited creature, and they bounded away quick as a flash. The others, agitated, turned to chase the doe; but she, with Eepersip on her back, had vanished.

"Whew, that was a narrow escape!" Eepersip whispered in one of the doe's long ears, as they lay down together.

The next day it rained hard. Eepersip's parents and their friends spent much time making plans for a day when they could go out. Mrs. Ikkisfield now made a suggestion.

"It is," she said, "very like the plan that we tried last night – namely, to find Eepersip while she is sleeping. But we must have more people, more people! If we can get some friends from the village at the foot of the mountain, they can drive the deer that we meet away from the people that are carrying Eepersip. In that way she cannot be saved by deer."

"That is true," said Mrs. Eigleen; "but, you know, often an angry herd of deer is a terrible thing to drive back."

"I know that," said Mrs. Ikkisfield. "But we might be able to keep them cool – keep them from getting angry. However, let's make some other plans now. That is not a very good one."

"I was thinking," said Mrs. Wraspane, "if we could only get Eepersip into a small fenced-in area where we could catch her. But I have it: let us find Eepersip in her sleep again, and carry her to the tent in a roundabout route through the woods, chopping the bushes as we go, where there aren't so many deer, and where it will be harder for them to rescue her."

"Great idea!" cried Mrs. Ikkisfield.

So that is what they all planned to do, the next sunny day.

*****

While they had been conversing in this manner, Eepersip had been sitting in the woods, with a little fawn and its mother for company, and she had been feeding the fawn handfuls of grass and gazing into its gentle eyes. Late in the evening it cleared off and there were promises of a beautiful day to- morrow. And so it was. The sun began to rise slowly, producing wonderful colors – first the most delicate shades of apple-blossom pink, darker on the horizon, and shading off into a pale buttercup yellow. And Eepersip, as she awoke, saw that the meadow was dotted with dark forms which could just be distinguished – the deer were all lying down.

Eepersip skipped up to the pool to get her morning drink, first spying all around and especially behind every tree. No one was to be seen, for no one was up yet. Eepersip drank her fill; then she breakfasted on the sweet root of the little three-leaved plant with a white blossom, her usual food. After that she went down to the meadow, beginning to dance and sing as soon as she got there. The deer were now beginning to rise, and as she danced she kissed each one.

When the sun had dried the raindrops and the dew, the families started out to the great field to see what they could discover. The first thing they saw when they got to the edge of the slope was Eepersip skipping around. Then they saw her dance off to the woods and gather some long green branches and blossoms. Very soon she came back to the field, went over to a sleeping doe, and crowned her with the branches; upon which the doe got up and licked Eepersip's cheek. She danced about in her delight. She was so beautiful, so graceful, that when her parents saw her they were amazed at the way in which her dancing and leaping had improved.

Now, during the days in which Eepersip had been growing wild she had made friends with another chipmunk, who was even more fond of her than the one by the pool had been. The Eigleens and their friends now saw him scutter out of the woods and frolic around Eepersip. Last of all they saw Eepersip lie down on the grass to gaze at the sky.

"This would be a splendid opportunity for catching her," muttered Mr. Ikkisfield to Mr. Eigleen, as they looked at her.

"Hm! that's just what I was thinking," whispered Mr. Eigleen in reply. "Suppose we go out in the field and try."

They all tiptoed down the slope and out into the field, where they immediately laid hands on Eepersip once more. She started violently and cried out to the doe who was near. The doe dashed up, but did not succeed in rescuing Eepersip, for Mrs. Ikkisfield ran to hold her back.

"Never mind Eepersip – Mr. Eigleen and Mr. Wraspane can do that. Hold back the deer!" thundered Mrs. Eigleen, a slow red rising to her face. They all flew at the poor creature, except the two who were holding the struggling Eepersip. Off fled the doe; and then the others could help with Eepersip. The doe ran on to get help from her mate. Back they came in no time, for a deer is one of the swiftest runners in the world. The buck flew at Eepersip's captors – just too late, for the others had succeeded in getting Eepersip safely into the tent.

But what could they do with her? How could they keep her securely? And, even so, if she was going to continue acting wildly; how much better off were they with her? This was a new question, which no one had thought of. But they decided that, if they could keep her safely, she would become tamed and civilized again. The question of security was the most important just then. Better go home immediately and take Eepersip with them, later returning for their tent and their belongings. This they did, locking Eepersip in the house while they were getting their things; and as they went they rejoiced.

But now all the deer of the field, knowing that Eepersip, their beloved queen, had been taken from them, put their heads together. They intended to rescue her while her father and mother were sleeping, if they could only find where she had been taken. While they were lying down and thinking about it, a fawn came running up and poked its mother. It had followed softly, and knew just where Eepersip was kept. They all lay down to wait for the coming of night. At last evening came, and the deer fell asleep, leaving a night-watchman to arouse them later when the full moon was at its zenith.

17

When the watchman signaled they arose and, with the little fawn leading, went down toward the Wraspanes' house. Eepersip was allowed to sleep out on the porch, but all its glass doors were closed and locked against her. The fawn led them straight to this place.

Eepersip could not go to sleep; she sat on the floor, whining softly in her misery. One of the bucks knocked gently on the glass door with his antler. Eepersip turned; a smile crept over her face at the sight of her beloved comrades. The buck, as softly as he could, broke one of the glass doors, wood and all. Then the deer, all except the fawn, bounded off to the field again.

The sound of breaking glass reached the ears of Mr. Ikkisfield, who was awake, all too late; for by the time he had wakened the others – which he did by shouting "Get up! Get up! Sounds like high doings out there!" – Eepersip, on the little fawn's back, had vanished toward the field. The families, when they got to the porch, found only the broken door. Though they heard trampling hoofs, they knew that it would be of no use to follow.

The families, after that adventure, were desperate; and they decided not to make any more plans just then, for winter was coming on rapidly, but to stay at the house until the next summer.

*****

As for Eepersip, well, she was mighty glad to have got away unhurt. Happy again, she was soon sound asleep in the woods on the edge of the field, cuddled up underneath the doe which had saved her before. She wasn't sure how to get along through the winter safely, but she had had such a splendid summer that she knew it would be foolish to give up her wild life now. She could manage somehow.

And so she did. She found that her parents had left her own heavy winter coat in the place where they had once found her sleeping; and this would be very helpful to her, she thought. She was also glad to realize that her parents, much though they wanted to get her back, didn't wish her to perish in the cold of winter. "They *are* nice people, after all" she thought to herself.

With the coat and the prospect of warmth, there came a delightful idea into her head. On the edge of the meadow there was an old dilapidated fox-hole. It was very large already; and after about ten days of hard work Eepersip found that the passages could be made exactly large enough for her to crawl into. The earth was so loose and moldy that it came away without difficulty. She crept down the tunnel a long way, digging as she went. Presently she came to a snug bedroom about five feet square and four and a half high, which was a little less than her own height. But she did not mind stooping, as long as she had this cunning room; besides, she could dig away the ceiling if she wanted to. The room was old and dirty, but Eepersip lined it entirely with grass. Digging around, in one corner she came upon a little packet made of leaves. Inside it were a few cordary-berry seeds. She wondered who had made this packet – who had lived in this burrow before her. A person, of that she was sure. These seeds had not by any means rotted; they were still as moist and sweet as ever, and Eepersip rejoiced to find them. Digging around some more, she discovered a small square block of wood. Lifting it up, she found great heaps of milkweed pods, kept from springing open by the pressure of the earth against them. She rejoiced in this too. There was enough of the milkweed to make a bed for herself. She covered the bed with her old dress, which she had kept all this time in case she should need it. Never was such a soft bed seen. In the burrow she also built several shelves of boards, and on these she heaped up more cordary berries and their seeds, which were just beginning to come.

The next day was the last of November. In the morning Eepersip, after a long sleep in the burrow, woke up to find the world white with the first snow. The entrance of the tunnel was placed at such an angle that never a flake found its way down in. Eepersip was delighted; she danced and skipped about, with the chipmunk at her heels.

The next day it stopped snowing, and the sun came out, shining dimly. Every snow-crystal sparkled like a diamond. Eepersip and the chipmunk dashed across the meadow and looked far, far down. Though ordinary eyes could not have seen to the end of this mass of glittering whiteness, Eepersip's could, and beyond all the icicles and snowflakes she saw the river calmly shining, blue as the sky. In its rippling surface Eepersip could see the very reflection of the sun breaking out through a cloud. The meadow was beautiful even when the sun was dim, but nothing to what it was now!

Eepersip could see every color of the rainbow reflected in each crystal – orange, purple, green, blue, red, and many, many iridescent tints. Full of joy, she looked down upon the river once more, through the glittering iridescence. The longer she looked, the better she could see the river. But at last the sun went in again; it had been out hardly long enough to melt one snowflake. Everywhere round Eepersip went the chipmunk's little footprints, for he had shared her delight. At last, when Eepersip wanted to go back to her subterranean shelter, the chipmunk hung back and whimpered. Eepersip saw that he wanted to stay; and, knowing that he could find his way, she left him behind and went back to the burrow herself.

But he didn't come back. She waited and waited and often called, but he did not appear. "What can have happened to my little friend?" she thought. At last she set out to look for him, calling as she went. She looked in every crevice, to see whether something had frightened him and he had plunged into some hiding-place. But she did not find him. At last, whistling and calling, she came near to where she had left him, on the edge of the meadow. Then what did she see in the snow but footprints – human footprints! Chippy's little tracks had started back in the direction of the burrow, but the strange footprints came towards his and overtook them – and at that point his suddenly left off. Then she discovered the others going down the hill again. It was only too clear – Chippy had been captured!

Eepersip sat down in the snow and wept. But suddenly she straightened up and became herself again. Why not follow those footprints down the hill and get her Chippy back? With a hopeful heart she dashed down, following the tracks. But she came into a small village, where she was afraid of being caught. She could not go on; so she went back.

Another idea! Why not follow the footprints some night, when there were not so many people around, and when, even if there were, she would not be seen so easily? But there was the question of being able to see the footprints in the dark. No, that would be impossible: the only thing to do would be to wait. For what? Eepersip had not the slightest idea.

The name of the people who had captured the chipmunk was Brunio. Mr. Brunio and his little twin daughters, Flitterveen and Caireen, had come up to the meadow with sleds and skis to slide. They had seen the chipmunk frolicking about, and had watched him impatiently.

"How I would like that little animal for my own!" said Flitterveen.

"He looks cold and hungry, Father," said Caireen. "Here, I have some crackers in my pocket. Let us throw them to him and see if he will eat them."

This they had done, and the chipmunk had been tempted. He had come up cautiously and nibbled at them. He loved Eepersip dearly. He had never received harm from one of those queer two-legged creatures. He trusted them. But, while he had been nibbling, Mr. Brunio had sneaked up quietly and taken him. Thus he had been captured.

*****

Eepersip was not able to free her little friend until the next spring. She had lived a rather lonely life without him through the winter, and one morning very early she decided to make a desperate attempt to rescue him. She went down the slope of the hill to the river, through grass wet with pearly dew-drops. She stole along the bank of the river, behind bushes as much as possible, so as not to be seen. Finally she came to a little wooden bridge, and across this she went. But from there she had no idea how to proceed. She looked all about her, bewildered, afraid among so many houses.

It was a heavenly morning. The sun rose and cast a sweet golden light over the earth. The grass sparkled as if with diamonds. A fresh spring breeze was blowing gently. Flowers grew here in the deep grass, and myriads of butterflies came flocking. But Eepersip stood forlorn and discouraged.

Suddenly a faint squeaking came to her. She darted toward the sound. O Eepersip, beware – not too fast! The squeaking came from one side of a dark brown house. Eepersip saw a small wire cage, and in it her little brown Chippy. Mr. Brunio had opened the squeaky door of the house and was coming out with Chippy's food. Eepersip saw him, and swerved aside into the shelter of a gigantic rose-bush before he saw her – just in the nick of time. It seemed like a long wait, but after a while Mr. Brunio went into the house again.

Looking cautiously about her, Eepersip tiptoed out, opened the door of the cage, seized Chippy, and sped off. Thus he was rescued; and Eepersip was happy indeed! As for the Brunios, they were very much distressed when they found out that the chipmunk was gone. By spying, they discovered some of Eepersip's strange habits. Then, early one morning, they took their little kitten – the twins had rather stupidly named her "White," for her color – up to the field where Eepersip had her home, let her go very near Eepersip's burrow, and then ran away quickly before the kitten could find them. Well, White didn't care much about being left in the dewy grass, bewilderedly shaking first one paw, then another. But presently Eepersip came out of her burrow with Chippy. Seeing the patch of white, Eepersip thought the kitten was an exceptionally late bit of snow left on the grass. But no, it certainly had not been there the last time she had looked. And then she realized that it was altogether too late for any snow. Darting up to it, she found the little kitten, so snow-white, with the blue-grey eyes like little moonstones, gazing pitifully up at her. Because she thought the kitten had been a patch of snow Eepersip named her Snowflake.

She took her, shivering with the wetness of the dew, into her burrow, and found, much to her surprise, that Chippy recognized her and sprang at her in great delight. The truth of the matter was that Chippy had often seen the kitten during his captivity, and had played many a happy game with her in his cage.

Caireen and Flitterveen had thought when they let the kitten go that Eepersip, seeing a new animal, would give them back Chippy. Not so! Eepersip would rather have two animals than one. Besides, she saw how dearly the two loved each other, and would not have parted them for anything now. The Brunios had been disappointed enough at losing Chippy – and now they had lost the kitten too!

It was now summer, and the Brunios – Mr. Brunio, Caireen, and Flitterveen – decided to climb Eiki-ennern Peak and try to get back their kitten. They wandered around a little while and at last came to a sunny place on the edge of the woods. It was a very grassy spot, all surrounded with blackberry-bushes just blossoming. Near its edge was Chippy asleep, and in the middle was Snowflake washing herself and playing with the dry oak-leaves that swirled about in the breeze. Snowflake started back a little at the sound of whispering voices, and then looked up. Eepersip was not there, for she had gone off to find some sweet bulbs and roots.

"Come on, White, dear!" called Caireen.

But Snowflake did not know her old name since Eepersip had changed it.

"Here, Sugar-bowl!" said Mr. Brunio. (He had got rather used to calling her that, because she loved sugar and had a habit of pawing into the sugar-bowl to get it.) This was a trifle more familiar, and she took a step forward.

"That's the way!" said Flitterveen, encouraging her. "Come on!" Snowflake took back the step.

They grew impatient; yet some of their calls were so encouraging that Snowflake could hardly resist creeping through the briers to their feet. Pretty soon she touched Chippy with her nose. He awoke, yawned two or three times, and, when he saw the people there, instantly pattered off into the woods. Now Snowflake sat very still, in spite of all their coaxing, for she knew that help was coming. And she didn't have long to wait, for in a moment Eepersip came running up with Chippy in her arms. With a beautiful leap she cleared the briers and, taking up Snowflake, cleared them again and vanished into the woods.

Life for Chippy and Snowflake was great fun during the time when Mr. Brunio, sometimes with the twins, was coming up to the brier-patch and trying to entice Snowflake away. In the afternoons, though the two little animals were glad to stay in the brier-patch, Eepersip generally took them along with her when she went anywhere, for she thought that possibly Mr. Brunio might come up with an ax to chop down the briers. In this Eepersip proved wise, for, about the third day that Mr. Brunio and the children had been coming up Eiki-ennern Peak to rescue Snowflake, Mr. Brunio did bring an ax. But this time Eepersip had taken the two little animals out with her; they had gone exploring, finding sweet roots and brilliant berries.

Eepersip spent that summer in continual fits of dancing, laughing, and merriment. She had never before been so happy. Every day she felt as though she loved the animals, birds, and butterflies– everything of Nature – more than the day before. She loved to see the same birds coming back this year. Above all she loved the delicate butterflies with wings of all colors. She would lie in the meadow for hours and watch what was happening. She could imagine miniature cities in the air, and saw little butterflies and birds constantly going and coming from them. There were cities on the ground, too, where orchestras of grasshoppers and crickets played in the grass.

She sometimes made up words for her melodies – little songs of Nature. She would sing them over and over, sometimes ringingly, sometimes in a murmur.

Buttercups are smiling To see the butterflies
Feathering so softly, Rainbowing the skies. . . .

The wind is snowing butterflies, Fairy golden showers;
Misty the air with dancing wings; The sun is raining flowers.

She told the deer that *she* felt like a butterfly, and that the wind was snowing *her* when she danced. And then she gave them handfuls of lush grass.

*****

At the end of that first winter Mrs. Eigleen began to feel ill. No one knew what was the matter with her. She spent the spring in continual weeping and hysterics. Towards

24

the summer she began to feel seriously ill. They had had several different doctors in to see her, but none of them could find out exactly what the matter was, for she refused to tell anyone anything, even though she said she herself knew. One afternoon she called her friends round her and bade them take her over to the meadow, where they would surely see Eepersip. They took her out, but never a trace of Eepersip did they see. And Mrs. Eigleen kept on having her fits of weeping all through the summer, even more frequently than before.

Now, by this time Mrs. Eigleen, her husband, and all her neighbors had found out that Eepersip had taken White away from the Brunios; for once they had been out in the field and seen Eepersip. She was crowned with a wreath on which butterflies were clustering in bunches, like grapes; and Chippy and Snowflake were frolicking about her. The Eigleens, the Ikkisfields, and the Wraspanes went down the meadow and to Mr. Brunio's house (for some of them knew the Brunios and recognized the kitten), and he related his adventures. That very afternoon they went back to the meadow and chased Eepersip, but they couldn't catch her, for she took up Snowflake and Chippy and mounted a doe, who bore them off like the wind.

The next day, they tried again: It was dawn, and Eepersip was lying in the center of the meadow with Snowflake and Chippy by her side. She had had her breakfast, but she lay on the grass watching the sun rise and send away the shadows to right and left, flushing the sky with delicate pink and yellow. The deer were still lying down. Eepersip heard a sound of voices talking, followed by a roar of laughter; and instantly, of course, she grew suspicious. She heard: "Mr. Wraspane, will you come with me?" "Certainly, Mr. Eigleen," "Mrs. Ikkisfield, you come with me. We are the ones that are not so skilled in slyness. We will go up on the hill and guard there." "All right, Mrs. Eigleen."

As Eepersip lay there in the field, two men broke out of the woods right near where she was lying. She sprang to her feet, caught Chippy and Snowflake in her arms, and ran. Before she could match up the two little animals, Mr. Eigleen was just able to seize her dress as she darted by him. But, of course, the fern that he caught hold of came out in his hand, and she ran along toward the hill – a foolish thing to do, for she had just heard that there were two people guarding it. Still, that was just about the only thing that she could do, for the other two, Mr. Ikkisfield and Mrs. Wraspane, had also come out of the woods and blocked her path.

Eepersip fled up on the hill and nearly ran into Mrs. Eigleen and Mrs. Ikkisfield. Mrs. Eigleen caught hold of Snowflake's tail, and Mrs. Ikkisfield stepped in front of Eepersip, who dodged desperately to one side, releasing her hold on the kitten to prevent its being injured.

But Eepersip was not going to give up her pet just yet. She sped down the hill, knowing that the others would soon be going to give the kitten back to the Brunios. Through the big field she ran, with Chippy clinging to her hair – down the other side of the slope to the river, along its banks, across the small bridge 'way down, and back to Mr. Brunio's house on the other side.

Eepersip looked all about her for some place of concealment. No one was in sight. Along the side of the house there was a forest of blackberry-bushes, which extended several yards and was unusually dense and towering. The luscious black-and-purple fruit was ripening, making it look even more sheltering and mysterious. This patch was also in such a position that it had to be passed to reach the front door, which was really on the side of the house. Eepersip was pleased to find such a convenient place. She sampled the berries with satisfaction, always taking pains to see that no one was coming. Then she wriggled inside and waited.

Presently they all came along, Mrs. Ikkisfield holding Snowflake. Eepersip had ready in her hand a little sharp-pointed stick. She pushed it through a tiny hole in Mrs. Ikkisfield's stocking. It hurt! Mrs.

Ikkisfield gave a little shriek of pain and dropped Snowflake, who instantly put her paw on a small fern which she saw – she couldn't see Eepersip, but the fern was very familiar! – and was pulled by Eepersip into the bush. When the people saw that, they knew, of course, who was near.

Eepersip started to crawl through the bush and out the other side; but she heard Mr. Eigleen whispering to the others to go around and stop her. While they were watching, Mr. Brunio, who had joined them, went back into the house and fetched a net. It was woven, of course, thick ropes, but the meshes were quite small enough to hold the kitten, and almost Chippy himself. (Mr. Brunio had once been a fisherman; he had retired, but he still had many nets with meshes of various sizes.) They put this net over the bush and pegged it down firmly, driving the pegs with the head of an ax which Mr. Brunio brought out. Then they retreated to a distance and watched.

Eepersip began working at the pegs, and the chipmunk and the kitten to dig at the base of each so that she might be able to pull them up more easily. The pegs were really too big for Eepersip's little hands to manage comfortably, but she didn't think of comfort in such danger as this, and she worked boldly at the pegs with her nimble fingers. After she had got two or three up, the Eigleens and their friends came forward, took those pegs, and put them down more firmly than before, so that Eepersip had to begin all over.

Although the people who were trying to capture Eepersip and the kitten were naturally becoming very hungry, they didn't like to leave the bush unguarded. But Mr. Brunio (who was exceptionally hungry) said that he had many more such nets, and that they could spread them all over the bush and hurriedly get luncheon. If they put them down very firmly, and ate rather fast, there wouldn't be much chance of Eepersip's escaping before they could get out again. So they spread four more nets over the bush and went in.

Now was Eepersip's chance, and she worked harder than ever. At last, with the aid of Chippy and Snowflake, who helped a lot by digging around the pegs, Eepersip got out of the first net and began tugging at the second. She didn't try to dig up the pegs of this one: instead, all three tried to dig under it, and at last they had made a hole large enough for Eepersip to crawl through. The fibers of the third net were rather rotten, so that Eepersip tore it easily. Each peg of the fourth and fifth nets came up at one mighty yank; Mr. Brunio and his helpers had put the last nets down in a great hurry, in order to get their luncheon. Then Eepersip, with the two little animals, fled from that dread place, across the bridge and back to the meadow, where she found a sheltered spot and slept.

*****

The three families were much disgusted with themselves for not catching Eepersip and the kitten; but they promised Mr. Brunio that they would try again. There followed a week of rainy weather, during which they made no attempts, but laid plans. As soon as the weather cleared, they tried one of these plans; and Snowflake had a narrow escape.

It was in the middle of the night. The families found Eepersip, with the two little animals, asleep on the meadow. They took the kitten from her arms. But as they did so, Eepersip herself woke up, screamed loudly, and rushed after them. Then they turned and came after her; and Eepersip was bold enough and angry enough not to run until she had rescued Snowflake. She came right up to her parents and seized Snowflake from the arms of the horrified Mrs. Eigleen. Then Eepersip ran – and fast, too!

When she came to the edge of the woods she made straight for a great pine. This tree she had climbed about in often, and she knew its every limb. In pitch dark she could find all its branches, and sometimes she trusted to her memory rather recklessly. She was as sure of this tree as of the ground, even at night. She loved it – she called it *her* tree. A tree was, perhaps, not the easiest place of concealment, but Eepersip thought that in this way she would not have to run all over the meadow in the dark – and she was very tired after her usual all-day playing.

There were no branches lower than seven feet up. Eepersip made one leap, caught hold of a branch, and swung herself up on to it. From that branch she mounted higher and higher until she reached the very top. It swayed gloriously, even under her light weight, but it didn't creak as if about to break. She sat up in the high crotch and looked at the people so far below, through a mass of black needles and a mighty thickness of strong limbs. It was a wonderful night. The sky was spangled with stars of vivid silver. Not a cloud was to be seen except on the western horizon, where a bank was piling up rapidly, silhouetted against the deep ultramarine of the sky, across which the Milky Way made a path of radiance. Eepersip, looking down among the powerful limbs, felt as if she were part of the familiar tree.

Poor Chippy and Snowflake were tired and sleepy after what they had just been through. Eepersip murmured kind words to them, while she thought of all that she had been through herself. She was not in the least dizzy, but she was tired, and she knew that she must not go to sleep up there.

Then she saw that Mr. Eigleen had started to climb the great tree. He got about half-way up, and then stopped. She remembered the place: it had been difficult for her, too. There was not a limb where he could put out a foot and step on it; the next one was at the level of his neck. The question was, how could he get on to this limb? He didn't have the strength to pull himself up to it the way Eepersip had done. He tried for a long time; but his caution proved too much for him. At last, in despair, he descended; and the people went away, leaving Eepersip in peace.

As soon as they were well out of sight and hearing, Eepersip came down in a series of leaps from limb to limb. At length she got to the bottom, where the last limb was seven feet from the ground. She braced herself as firmly as she could on this, and then she jumped. It was a marvelous jump in the dark, and she landed on the ground unhurt, though very tired and covered with bits of bark. "My, that was a dreary adventure!" she said sleepily, as she crawled off to find a place to sleep.

*****

Eepersip saw no more of the Brunios or her parents and she decided that they had given up chasing her and Snowflake for the winter – a winter which she and her two friends spent undisturbed, playing with the leaves and shadows.

It was spring – spring before the third summer that Eepersip was to spend wild – and the golden sun melted away the last patches of snow from off the bare rocks and from round the pool, where it had lodged between them. It was warm, although a wind was blowing – the delicious wind of spring. This marvelous spring air made her blood course quickly. She felt extremely happy and dancy. Her body seemed to her lighter than ever, in spite of its strength. Her spirit was so joyous that she could not express it in action; she had to let part of it out in song. But song, however light and happy, could not quite express Eepersip's feeling. She danced, and she sang, and she leaped aloft for joy.

As the season advanced, she crowned herself with sweet-smelling flowers, and the butterflies came and lit on them. She went up to the pool wearing her fluttering crown, and there she saw the flowers that had come to bloom. There was iris purple and gold – huge blossoms which reminded Eepersip of the ocean as she had seen it, so far away, on the first day of her wanderings. In a soft bed of green moss she found a little pink-and-white flower that she didn't know, bell-shaped and very fragrant. There were wild-rose-buds there, too, and never had Eepersip seen so many butterflies as were on those roses. They bordered the tiny beach, mingled with the tenderly uncurling green ferns. The delicate red leaf-buds on the maple-trees were now developing into tiny emerald leaves. And there were ever so many other treasures of Nature there.

Eepersip played little happy games with all the creatures of the field. One game she played with the crickets. A cricket would be hiding in a certain place, and when Eepersip danced by he would buzz out of the grass into her face; she would pretend to be startled and would run from the spot. She played another game with the grasshoppers. One would be hiding, and Eepersip would come dancing by with her eyes shut. Then the grasshopper would whirr out of the grass and alight on her hand. When she opened her eyes she would shake her hand and try to get rid of him, all in fun, of course. Then she played two lovely games with the happy butterflies. She would let a butterfly alight on her hand, to which she would then give a violent jerk, so that the butterfly was sent sailing into the air; then, without a motion of the wings, he would come sailing back to Eepersip's hand. This they would do again and again. When she tired of this game, Eepersip would crown herself with the sweetest flowers she could find, and then flocks of butterflies would try to alight on her wreath as she danced. There were never enough flowers for all of them; some were always fluttering around Eepersip's head, trying to find a nestling-place, and others were safely folded in the blossoms.

One of the thrilling hours of Eepersip's happy life that summer was when she lay in the meadow watching the sky and all the swallows circling. Snowflake and Chippy were frolicking gayly in the short, dry grass, chasing leaves. Now Chippy snuggled up to Eepersip. Snowflake kept on playing; she was crouched on her little white belly, playing with a dry brown leaf, and when it drifted beyond her reach she would spring after it. Eepersip watched her in a dreamy way. Now Snowflake cast the dead leaf away, having torn it to shreds, and played with other things. Sometimes she would rear herself up into the air; at other times she would run with little tripping steps over to Eepersip, as if something had frightened her; again, she would rush round and round Eepersip in a wide circle, and finally she would settle down to play with another dead leaf. It made Eepersip glad to hear the kitten's little pattering feet on the grass; she knew how madly Snowflake was frolicking, but she did not share in the play-instead, with a dreamy happiness, she watched the sky.

Another day in the summer was even happier. It was in July, and Eepersip was lying in a part of the meadow where there weren't many deer so that the grass was long, soft, and green instead of stiff and short. Snowflake and Chippy were frolicking around in it, but again Eepersip was not thinking of them. She was thinking of the swallows that flew over her, and the way the sun shone on their breasts, making them glitter like silver. The crickets were chirping and the grasshoppers were accompanying them, and they were both very happy. The frogs croaked bass songs from the pool – the cool, green frogs! The birds were singing merrily and the butterflies passed over Eepersip's head in flocks – butterflies of white and purple and blue and yellow, little ones of copper-green, and big ones of orange and red. Some of them flew with short, quick flirts of the wings, others with long strokes which swept them through the air. The gauzy dragonflies, too, flew over her. Everything thrilled Eepersip's happy, tireless eyes.

The bees hummed their way low over the long green grass, and Chippy and Snowflake leaped high in the air when they passed. Eepersip had taught the two little animals not to catch the creatures of the field, and before long all the birds loved Snowflake – something that few kittens have yet attained. But Snowflake and Chippy liked to pretend to catch the bees, and sometimes they went so far as to hold them on the ground with their paws, very gently, not hurting them at all. Snowflake and Chippy lay in the grass, reaching and touching anything that took their fancy. When the wind blew they would leap up at the clover-blossoms that nodded. They played hide-and-seek, leaping over the grasses and chasing each other in and out of their hiding-places. The long grass offered a splendid place of concealment. Chippy would scurry behind a big sheltering tuft, seeming to Snowflake to have vanished in mid-air. Snowflake would poke about and run in such bewildering circles that it tired them looking at each other. Soon they would get so mixed up that they wouldn't know which of them was supposed to be hiding, and it often happened that they were both hiding at the same time, or both searching.

This was for Eepersip the happiest of that summer's hours in the field. Something fresh and fragrant in the air made breathing a delight; it almost lifted her off the ground, and she let forth a glorious burst of song.

31

*****

It was a cold, frisky day in October, and Eepersip, even in her warm coat, had to keep moving.

Snowflake and Chippy were frolicking and playing games with each other. Eepersip had taught them how to shake hands, and this they were practicing. A leaf had settled on Snowflake's head like a brown crown, and she was trying vigorously to get it off. But no, the leaf was curled firmly around her small, dainty ears. She got wilder and wilder in her amusing efforts. She dashed round and round. She reached after it with her forepaws. All in vain! She could not get rid of that persistent leaf. But there! a gust of cold wind sent it flying from her head, to be instantly lost in a whirl of others which the wind had started up.

Snowflake dashed among them madly, and played with them, trying to catch them all at the same time. But at last she stopped her foolish efforts and came quietly back to rest.

In November the first snow of the winter fell. The flakes came thick and fast, like white and silver butterflies dancing, flying. Eepersip took them in her hands and noticed how each flake had its own shape, which was never found again. During that day in October Snowflake had worn a brown crown of a dead leaf, but now she wore a white one. The snow didn't show much on the white fur of the kitten, but Chippy's autumn brown was soon covered with a mossy blanket of it. The flakes whirled down thicker and faster than ever and Chippy tried to jump at them all. The playmates could hide in the snow now, for if they got far enough apart they couldn't see each other. They tried to capture the snowflakes, but they found that this made their paws even wetter.

In spite of all this merriment, Eepersip had a slightly sad feeling in her heart. The night before, she had seen the sea; and it had looked so glorious that she felt as if – as if she would like to go to it. She loved the meadow so much that this would be almost impossible for her. Yet she knew that in spite of her love for the meadow, her longing for the sea would grow, and that one day she must leave her present home. All this made her rather sad. But she tried to be happy – to share the joy of her two little friends, and the joy of having the little fairy things come whirling down upon her. She played all day in the meadow with her friends, and when the evening fell they went back to the burrow and slept in peace till morning.

In this way the winter passed. Every evening at sunset Eepersip would go over to the edge of the meadow and gaze long upon the sea, with the brilliant sunset colors reflected in it. And each time she looked it seemed so beautiful, so beautiful! and each time she tried to go to it, it seemed as if the ground of the meadow was a great magnet to her feet.

The spring came, and with it the flowers and leaves.

One night Eepersip woke up to find the full moon as if hanging in the sky. A few faint stars could be seen. She tried to go to sleep, but could not. At last she got up from her bed of moss. The dew lay thick on the grass, which slushed deliciously against her bare feet. All entranced with the beauty of the night, she ran lightly over to the spot where she often had a view of the sea. And she beheld it with the full moon reflected in it – a globe of soft silver, shimmering and quivering in the unstill waters. This time it was too much for Eepersip. She could stand it no longer – her heart gave way. She decided that the next morning she would satisfy her longing.

And so, just after dawn, she left her beautiful home in the field and journeyed toward the ocean. She went to the edge of the meadow with a herd of deer daintily tripping after her. She turned and cried: "Good-bye, O deer! for probably I shall never see you again." She kissed the ground of the meadow, and she wept to think that she was leaving it; but she knew that her love for the sea had become greater than her love for the meadow. And then she went away – sadly, yet happy at the prospect of a new and beautiful life by the foaming, churning rocks and the white-capped waves.

CHAPTER II

THE SEA

*Your flashing waves hold out
their arms to me – I entangle myself
in their silver hair,
And ride with them to catch the wind.
The sun trails bright jewels in the water,
And laughs because I cannot touch them.*

AS EEPERSIP JOURNEYED ON, the meadow grew dimmer in her mind, and the memory of how the sea had looked grew brighter. She couldn't see it now, for she was in a valley; but she knew that she was going in the right direction. The spring breeze was blowing; it was not cold, and the breeze stirred the air gently, so that it wasn't hot. Occasional whiffs from the meadow came to Eepersip with that breeze; but when she had gone about two miles this fragrance ceased.

That afternoon she came into a great forest where strange, mysterious shadows passed back and forth in a frightening way. She hurried on as fast as she could, but she had to spend a night in it – one alarming, terrible night. The next day she came out, torn

34

and bedraggled with lighting her way through the dense thickets. Several times she had to cross rivers – some of them without a bridge, though luckily none of these was over her depth. Another day had passed. Nightfall found her wearily climbing a very high hill. The reflection of the moon showed her where the ocean was. It seemed hardly any nearer than before!

The third morning she descended into a rich and fertile valley. A small brook was winding down it, and where the weeping willows dipped into the current it bubbled and sang. This valley was the broadest that Eepersip had yet gone through. But after a long time she came out of it against a high, precipitous cliff. Up the side of this she climbed, digging her toes into the cracks between the rocks. At last she got to the top; and a long, weary climb it had been. She was now on a grassy hill where bloomed daisies shining like stars, and little buttercups of gold. There were butterflies, too, with brilliant wings, and they hovered and fluttered over the flowers. And lo! there was the ocean, nearer now, with the sun shining on it; and Eepersip could see the surf rolling and foaming. Shrill cries pierced the air – the cries of birds, of sea-gulls swooping inland in wide circles. And as she went on through the waving grass she could smell the delicious salt air of the sea.

But, alas, she met with a hindrance. Between her and the coast there was a valley extending for miles, and poor Eepersip would have to clamber down a precipitous cliff, through the valley, and up another cliff. Down she went, rather unwillingly, but knowing that she would get there sometime. At last she came to the bottom. It wasn't so bad down there – there was a lovely lakelet at which she refreshed herself with a drink; it was grassy, and there were flowers. But it was stiflingly hot. There was a patch of pine woods here and there, but it was hot even in the shade of the great trees.

She stumbled on in the almost blinding heat, clambering up the other great precipice – the wall of the valley. From the top she looked down, and, seeing again that ponderous cliff, she wondered how she could ever have got up it. Then she lay down on the grass, and in a moment was asleep.

When she awoke, the strong wind was blowing again. It made her almost fly through the cold, salty air. Before her was the long-sought ocean, with the waves rolling and the gulls swooping, diving, and screaming. She flew; her feet could not stay still. She was tired no longer – she didn't feel the smallest effects of her wearisome journey.

Suddenly she heard a sound – the magical sound of the waves as they crashed on the rocks. In they would come, pounding, roaring, breaking upon the shore. The foam and spume would fly back and leap up into the air. Everything sounded strange – stranger than anything Eepersip had ever heard. No words can describe what she imagined. She never had had such a lot of emotions in her head at the same time. She tried to describe them to herself, but soon gave it up as useless. She thought: "Here I am; I see it; you don't need to tell me about it!" And then she realized that she was alone, knowing in her own mind what it was like, yet unable to stop wishing that she could describe the hollow, ringing sound. Was she becoming homesick? No! it was sheer delight.

For a moment she paused. Then she bounded through the yellow sand, and, ever going faster and faster, she came to the edge of her sea. Her longing had been fulfilled.

This beach was almost overhung at one end by a great shelf of rock. The sand was glistening with shells of all colors and bordered with sea-weeds washed up. Tiny sand-pipers' tracks ran all over it.

Eepersip stayed there a long time, gazing into the waves, gazing at everything.

The rock-ledge at one end of the beach had been catching her eye for some time. She watched how fearlessly the gulls plunged on quivering wings, down, down, then rose again, covered with silvery drops, to fly here and there. Then she would look back at the little precipice. She thought: "*I* cannot fly! *They* do it from the air, but I cannot. I can do it from the precipice! Why not?" Then, aloud: "I *will* be a bird – I *will* do it!"

She walked back to the point where the cliff towered from the beach. She climbed up. She selected, in the water so far below, a place that was free from the treacherous-looking rocks. Then, swaying her arms a moment and plucking up high courage, she gave a flying leap and landed in the deep water.

Another miracle! She had never had a chance to swim before, but somehow she did it naturally now. It was an instinct in her to kick with her legs and throw out her arms in the right way. Fortunately she had landed in the place without rocks. Shaking herself in imitation of the gulls, so that silvery drops flew from her in all directions, she began to swim about. She played in the water for a long time, entranced, singing as she had never done before even in the meadow. After a while she came out, all shining, laughing and dancing. But it was then too late in the day to play anymore; so she lay down on the sand, well out of reach of the tide, and slept, with the murmuring of the sea in her ears all night.

*****

It had been high tide; but the tide was now going out, and near the beach the tops of the great jagged rocks were appearing. To Eepersip, who had never before been near the ocean, these things which happened every day were strange and delightful, and she could not look at them enough. Each wave was pure blue, topped and trimmed with spray. As the waters drew back Eepersip had to retreat; for the low tide revealed more and more rocks, and the spray that hit upon them flew back farther and farther.

Gradually they were left bare and dry, and Eepersip arranged sea-weeds and sea-plants in the little pools left in their hollows. When, at last, high tide came in, she sorrowed to watch them become part of the sea again. But she knew, of course, that when the tide went out other pools would be left – perhaps more than there had been before.

Among the rocks at the back of the beach Eepersip found a pool made by leaping spray from a storm. She trimmed it with sea-weeds of brown and green. She took some of the dried low-tide snails from the rocks around it and cast them into the sea. With her hands she caught some sluggish yet pretty little fishes and put them into her pool. As she was doing this she noticed how the tide was coming in – she had been so intent upon her task that she hadn't seen it. It was now almost up to her. She stopped what she was doing and watched it anxiously, afraid that it was going to reach her pool. But, to her great joy, it didn't. The waves lapped at it as if they wanted it very much, but they couldn't quite touch it; and Eepersip, worried no longer, continued her happy playing.

In this way the days passed, with something new all the time. But she did not forget her little pool. She tended it, putting in fresh plants and rocks, and replacing a fish if it died.

She slept in a crevice in the rocks at the end of the beach. There was a tunnel under the rocks that the water had cut; if she crept to the farther end, no tide could reach her. There was a spring in the pasture in back of the beach, about a hundred yards away, and there Eepersip got her supply of fresh water. It made a merry brooklet which ran bubbling down a small hill and into the sea. When it was stormy she had a habit of merely snuggling under the rocks as far as she could go, to watch the glistening white-caps and listen to the crashing surf. But before she had seen many storms she stayed out when they weren't too severe, and sometimes played about in the waves – and she liked to be ducked.

*****

In her explorations along the shore one day Eepersip found a great raft, made from interlacing twigs and plastered over with clay and pitch. Here and there great water-soaked ropes bound it firmly. It had been washed up on the shore, and, from a long period in the sea, had become terribly slimy and water-logged. Eepersip hauled it to the water to see if it would hold her weight, but it sank immediately. So she let it dry off in the sun for a long time; and at last, when it had become quite dry, she tried again. This time it held her. It started drifting off to sea with her on it, but she quickly slipped off and took it to shore again. A few days afterward Eepersip found a board, about three feet long and broad enough to serve perfectly as a paddle.

That was what she had wanted. She hauled the raft out to her depth; climbed on to it, took the paddle, and pushed off merrily.

Under strong strokes the water whirled and rushed, and the raft pushed through it. Sometimes she came to a sand-flat, and again to such a deep place that when she looked down all she could see was menacing shadows. Once the raft came into a shoal of carmine-colored fishes with very long pointed fins. Of course, they scattered in all directions as she came amongst them.

When she had started it was dawn. By midday, with the help of a favorable wind, she was out of sight of land. Then she saw that, if she were going to get back to the beach by evening, she must hurry and use her remaining daylight in that direction. So she turned about, with great difficulty because of the wind, and then she started homeward. But everything that had before been favorable was now against her; with her clumsy craft she could make no headway, and the waves were rising higher all the time. So she gave up, thinking that possibly the wind would soon change or calm down altogether. But this did not happen.

She was dashed about wildly, ever going farther from land, and seeing nothing save the unlimited expanse of rough water. Yet, even in her fright, she enjoyed it. She was not hurt at all, and she had only to cling tight to the raft. The sensation of being so dashed about and of riding up and down on the waves was glorious.

All the same, when it began to grow darker, darker, the wind remaining steady, she began to wish she had not ventured forth, but had stayed in shelter and safety at her little beach. She had always had great fun watching the storms, the high spray, the wind-tossed gulls; but now she saw that she had wished for rather too much.

It became steadily blacker, and still she was borne on, making no resistance now, for she saw how useless it was. By the faint remaining light from where the sun had set, she saw ahead of her a dark pointed object rising out of the water. She knew that it was a rock; and, afraid of being dashed against it, she began resisting with her paddle. Extreme fright made her strokes powerful, and she actually managed to slow up the raft a little. She came gently against the edge of the rock, fastened her raft to it by means of one of the ropes, and climbed up to its peak. From there, the sea, with its wild waves, was like the sky, full of weird cloud-caves, fringed with light from a hidden moon.

She looked for a long time; she looked steadily. And then, not far off, she saw a dark mass which, outlined against the deep blue of the night sky, appeared to be land – blessed land! She realized that the waves were going straight toward it. With a cry of joy, she unfastened her raft, leaped upon it, gave a useless push with her paddle, and went on.

Soon she came to the shore – a smooth beach. She pulled up her raft, well out of reach of the advancing tide, and started for the bushes to find a place to sleep. For the first time since night had fallen, she noticed the wondrous beauty of the moon, almost full, and the stars that showed faintly their silvery faces. She crawled in among the bushes, and, watching all these lovely things and listening to the soft murmuring of the waves, which were now calm again, she fell into a deep, delicious sleep.

*****

The next day the sea was absolutely calm. The sun was shining brilliantly on the water, making it dance and sparkle. Even Eepersip, who was so accustomed to waking in a different place from where she had been yesterday, was surprised to find herself where she was, and she had to rub her eyes hard to make sure that she was not dreaming. Then the whole adventure came back to her – the raft, the windy night, the raging sea, and the happy landing on this shore. There was her raft lying on the beach just where she had left it.

She got up and started to explore along the beach. But suddenly she stopped short in her tracks; for there, covered with climbing vines and bordered with bright little flowers, was a cottage – a little cottage in the midst of its forest of green leaves and bushes. Beautiful though it was, for a moment tears came to Eepersip's eyes. Exactly so had her own cottage looked; through all these years she had remembered it – just how it was in every detail. But this recollection soon passed away, in the dismay of realizing that she had come to an inhabited place. It was all so beautiful – she had wanted to stay and explore – and her hopes were crushed!

She stood stock-still for a long time, looking at the cottage. Nothing stirred within. Everything was quiet – oh! so quiet. Stealthily as a mouse Eepersip crept toward it, opened the door, and went in. A house, a detested house – one of those houses that she had run away from. Everything came back to her – those foolish coverings on the floors which they called carpets, at the windows those useless decorations called curtains. To think of it! when there was a carpet so much lovelier of green grass or of white sand – and no windows to be curtained!

It was a delightful little room, all the same, with a brownish woolly carpet, a small fireplace, and little blue curtains of a delicate material. It was quite deserted, so she decided not to let it bother her.

A small back door opened into the lovely woods at the back of the house. Quickly Eepersip made her way out into the open; and everything looked twice as lovely as before. How light it was, with all the world a window, instead of those silly little peep-holes fringed about! How much more glowing everything was! Oh, nothing in a house could compare with the world of light that Eepersip lived in!

Out here, the sunbeams made shadows wherever they struck; the birds twittered; the ripples lapped the shore caressingly. Otherwise all was still. But she was not thinking of the sea: she had decided to explore the woodland, for she felt, in a way, that it was her home. Following a little winding path, she came through a grove of white pines carpeted with needles and dotted with gnome-like toadstools of red and yellow, looking very bright and mysterious in that shady place.

They were, to Eepersip, like the traces of some elfin revel, perhaps thrones of precious mineral. There were great boulders, too, covered with grey-green lichens, some bearing aloft tiny cup-like blossoms of pearly grey – the cups from which the feasters had drunk their flower-wine. Seeing a lighter place ahead, she knew that she was coming out of the pine grove. A Hood of pale green radiance greeted her, as she stepped out of the dimness of the woods into a meadow. White and yellow butterflies were fluttering over it in great flocks, with wings shining.

Eepersip could hear birds chirping and singing. She passed on through the meadow and came again into woodlands, so thick now that hardly a sunbeam could penetrate the dense canopy of leaves.

After a while she emerged into a clearing. In the middle of it there was a pool, almost entirely surrounded with dark green moss, very soft, overhung by a boulder. It, too, had a covering of moss. A tiny stream flowed silently and mysteriously into the pool, which was so dark that Eepersip could just see its floor of dark sand. On the bottom grew strange star-leaved plants, and small fishes were nibbling them. It was all very strange and magical, it was so silent.

Eepersip stayed looking at this pool for a long time, and then she decided to follow the little brook which was trickling into it and see where it came from. She followed it through deep woodland for about three miles. All this way it was sluggish. Then the land changed abruptly; and Eepersip realized that she was climbing a steep and rugged hill. She went up and up on a rough path. It was very hard climbing, and she was becoming tired. At last she got to the top, and her happy eye looked back upon the way she had come.

She saw from that high perch the pool, into which she knew the little brook was trickling; the blotches which were clumps and patches of dark forest; the field, a mass of sparkling green light, a brilliant illumination to the gloomy pine forests around it; the cottage, a tiny brown speck in the distance and the sea, the billowing sea, with the spots of foam, the towering waves, and that green color which the waves show when they are agitated. She could even see the gulls, no bigger than flies to her, swooping about; but she was too far away to hear their shrill, excited screams. Long and steadily she looked. And then – the strangest thought Eepersip had ever experienced came to her happy mind. "Forgetfulness!" she whispered to herself. "Oh, I loved it so! and then, when it happened that I came to the woodlands again, why – I forgot it. I must go back instantly. But I am *so* tired!"

Each wave seemed to bring a pain to Eepersip's heart, as she watched the sea, like emerald, stretching away until it seemed to meet the blue sky. Suddenly she sprang to her feet and started down like a wild deer. Tearing through the woodlands, through the dense thickets and the brambles, she came out at last by the pool. But she had no eye for all its beauties; she had no mind but for the sea. She rested a second; then she was on her feet again, plunging, rearing, fighting her way through the woods. She came again, in the depths of exhaustion, into that pool of light, the meadow. Unable to move, she sank down in the delicious soft grass and watched the butterflies, like winged jewels, swooping above. Then she fell into a deep, heavy slumber.

She was awakened by shrill cries which pierced the air. Looking up, she saw a flock of gulls with their long, narrow wings, the color of foam, winging their way toward the sea. Then she remembered that she, too, was supposed to be winging her way toward the sea, and she cried: "O happy birds, I would I were among you, to go with such flashing speed!" It seemed to her that the sea was in her care, and that she, through foolish forgetfulness, had wandered off from it – wandered off from her guarding, leaving it to the mercy of the beasts. Of course, if she had thought a moment she would have seen how out of proportion this was, but she could do nothing but blame herself, and fancy a terrible monster who would come and drink it all up in her absence. And she began fighting and struggling against her tiredness, until, with one desperate effort, she managed to start running again. Then there was no stopping! Her old strength seemed to come back, the strength which she had had before starting her woodland explorations the result, as she thought now, of a foolish desire. Once she had started running again, her feet winged with a great longing, she sped along the ground.

Soon she passed the cottage; and then – there was her sea again, just as she had left it, with the waves beating the sandy shore. The gulls were screaming and diving; everything was excited and trembling. With a cry of ecstasy, Eepersip sprang into the waves.

*****

Many happy days Eepersip spent here, living in the vicinity of the hated little cottage. Since she had come to the sea she had worn a mermaid dress of sea-weeds, fastened at the neck by a white shell with a hole through it. Her favorite play was with the waves. She could swim now, even under water, with a speed that surprised herself, and she dived gracefully from all the rocks that she came upon. But it was watching the sea that fascinated her more than anything else. She would sit for hours at a time on the rocks and listen to the waves bellowing beneath her. Sometimes, when they were very high she would go down on the low rocks and shout with delight when the white spray rushed along and whirled itself up into her face. The waves would wash her over and over and play with her in their salty hands, and, though they seemed rough and wild, something always guided her away from the treacherous rocks which they headed for.

But she was born to wander, and it was not long before she was off on her explorations again. One sparkling day when the sun danced and glimmered on the little ripples, Eepersip started to explore the shore-line. Every sun-sparkle made her feel happier and happier and every breath of salty air lighter, until at last she thought she must rise up into the air on strong wings. After exploring quite a while and finding nothing unusual, she sat down on a rock. Her auburn curls goldened in the sunlight and her brown eyes sparkled.

After she had rested a while, watching the swooping sea-gulls, she decided to collect shells. She went along the beach some way, picking up shells and pebbles. But soon she tired of this and, feeling very hot, flung herself into the sea and played a while in the shallow water. Soon she thought that she would like to take a long swim, and she started out rapidly.

The waves came in higher and higher and brought with them great flocks of gulls sweeping around in wide graceful circles and uttering strange wild cries. Eepersip went on a long way until she saw a great rock ahead, draped with sea-weeds of a dark green which were floating up and down with the motion of the waves. There were many crabs and snails caught in them. She was borne forward to the rock in a mighty wave, and, clinging to it hard, she waited until the wave drew back before climbing up. After she had rested some time she noticed a shoal of shining little fishes down in the water. Some were gold, some silver, and some had bands of dark blue. They all had ruby eyes. She watched them for a long time, lying on her stomach on the rock. She observed how they nosed down and fed on the oozy sea- plants on the bottom, which were covered with silver oxygen-bubbles. Also she could see, 'way down there, lovely bright corals of all colors. The water was rather muddy, but there was a current coming in underneath, and before long it was perfectly clear. The rock was tremendous, spreading out beneath the surface and going down, down, all covered with slime and sea-weeds. Eepersip was fascinated watching those little fishes, she cared for nothing else. How long might she have watched them if the tide had not been rising and rising? Now it was touching her dress when a ripple larger than the others came in. And now – a flash of lightning down there in the shadows! Eepersip could not realize what had happened.

Then she thought: a great brownish-green fish had shot into the middle of the shoal, seized one of them, and carried it off. It was so quick that Eepersip could not think, until sometime after it was all over, what had really happened.

She swam to the shore, but, to her surprise, it was quite a different shore from where she had started. She wondered where she was. She landed on a beach of white sand, so fine that it was impossible to hold. It was covered with shells of all colors. These interested her for a long time, and she piled up the whole beach with heaps of them that she had collected, and had a beautiful time playing with herself until–

She saw some footprints! *Footprints!* They came down on the beach and apparently into the water, then out again, and disappeared in the woods on a narrow path which Eepersip had not noticed before.

But she was not interested in where they went to or where they came from. Her only thought was to get away – away. It was then too late to go out in the sea again – that is, far from shore. The sun was about to set. She would spend the night there, and then she would wander again. So she lay down and went to sleep.

*****

The next morning when she woke up she was not alone. A little golden-haired boy with sky-blue eyes was looking at her. They looked at each other for a long time.

"Who are you?" he ventured at last.

Here was a puzzler. "Eepersip Eigleen," she answered. "I mean," she added doubtfully, "I *was*." "Who are you now, then?"

"I don't know exactly." "Why don't you?"

"I haven't any name now. I'm just somebody. Have *you* any name?" "Yes – Toby – Toby Carrenda."

"Do you live here in the woods?" "Yes."

"In a house?"

He looked at her curiously a moment; then he said: "Yes, of course – don't you?" "NO!"

"How funny!"

"Yes, it is." With a little reluctance – "Will you play with me?"

Strange: here was Eepersip, who detested people, asking a little boy to play with her! It was simply that she, not having seen any children for a long time, was fascinated by this small boy who seemed so unafraid of her and so natural.

They wandered together on the beach and picked up shells. Then Eepersip asked the little boy if he liked to swim.

"Yes," he said, "But do you think I'd better?" "Yes – why not?"

"All right."

So he took off all his clothes and went in with her, and they splashed each other and had a lovely time. Eepersip wanted to make him a mermaid dress, but there was no sea-weed right there and she didn't want to leave him. So they went into the woods to find some ferns to make him a nymph dress. She found a beautiful ferny glade, and sat down and began to weave ferns together, talking to him at the same time. When it was all done he was delighted.

"But, please," he said, "can't I have a shell, too?"

He touched the shell strung up on her sea-weed dress. They looked all over the beach, and at last they found another shell with a hole all the way through. Then he was entirely content.

They went into the woods together and picked flowers, and Eepersip showed him how to make fern dresses and how to weave wreaths of flowers. They went into a grove of unlit white pines and danced there together. Finally the little boy said: "I'm hungry, Eeserpip."

"It's *Eepersip*," she said, "but it doesn't matter much. I'll find you something to eat." After a while they found some flame-colored berries, and then Eepersip dug up some white roots of which she was fond.

The boy said: "This is jolly, it is. Is this the way you get your food?" "Always," she said.

They played a while longer, and then someone called.

Eepersip had a strange feeling at that moment. She could not help feeling a certain reluctance when she had first played with him; then she had decided that he could not have anything to do with the civilized people she hated so. He must be separate from them, perhaps even a wild thing like herself. She felt a sensation of horror when this strange voice sounded. Then he was not alone – then he lived in a house with other people!

Startled, she cried: "Who's that?" "My mother," he answered.

"Then you don't live here all by yourself?" She had a bitter feeling of disappointment. "Oh, no."

"I *wish* you did." This escaped her before she could think. Strange, that some magic power in this child had already made her say as much as she had said.

"I must go now," he said sorrowfully. "But I'll be out this afternoon – I guess."

Eepersip fell on her knees in front of him and said entreatingly: "Will you do something for me?" "I will – maybe."

"Don't tell *anybody* about me." "Why?"

"Never mind why, but don't, will you?" "I want to."

"Then I won't play with you anymore."

"All right, Eepersip. I won't." She looked at him doubtfully. "I *promise* you I won't.

Good-bye. I like you."

*****

Eepersip was delighted with her little friend. She waited anxiously for him to come out. Presently he came.

"Eepersip," he said, "will you swim with me again?"

They went in again, and this time Eepersip showed him how to swim, by holding him up while he kicked with his arms and legs. After a long time he could swim a little bit by himself; and then Eepersip took him to some rather high rocks and showed him how to jump in. At first he wouldn't do it alone; she took his hand and they jumped in together. After that he did it alone, and screamed with laughter when he came up. Then Eepersip showed him how to go in head first, and he had so much faith in her that he tried it right off. Although he went rather flat, he liked it very much. The next time Eepersip bent him 'way over before he went in, and he straightened out and hit the water clean as an arrow. That was much better, he said.

Eepersip asked him what his mother had said about the fern dress, for he had gone in so quickly that he had forgotten his own clothes. He said that she had asked him about it, and he had said that he found it. Eepersip thanked him for not telling about her.

But she was discovered in spite of her caution. One day when they were playing in the woods, Mrs. Carrenda came out and found them. Eepersip dashed for the waves immediately, in spite of the fact that Toby's mother called: "Don't run away, little girl; I won't hurt you!"

But Toby began to cry bitterly. "Why did you send her away, Mother?" "I didn't, Toby. She ran as soon as I came. Who is she?"

That Toby did not answer. There were two instincts equally strong struggling within him – one to obey his mother, and the other to do what the strange girl asked him to with the threat of refusing to play with him if he did not.

"I can't tell you, Mother," he said courageously.

It would have been as true if he had said "I don't know," for he knew nothing but her name, after all. However, he never stopped to think that knowing her name was not all there was to knowing *her*.

Mrs. Carrenda wisely pursued the matter no further; but she determined to keep watch.

46

Eepersip was much more cautious after this. She was always on the lookout. Several times Toby asked her why she didn't want to be seen. But she would not answer him. She was, however, very kind in all other respects. Several times Mrs. Carrenda found Toby playing with her, but never spoke or let him know. She saw that Eepersip played nicely with him and that they liked each other much; so she did not interfere. Once, however, she put her hands suddenly on Eepersip's shoulders from behind and said kindly: "Little girl, don't be afraid of me."

Eepersip sprang to her feet, stared wildly a moment, and then dashed off straight to the sea. But for fear of making Toby very unhappy, Mrs. Carrenda never questioned him about her.

She and her husband had many anxious conferences together. Her husband thought that it was exceedingly risky to let Toby play so unwatched with Eepersip, but Toby's mother did not feel that way at all. Then they talked over the matter of who she was.

One day Eepersip was peeping into the house to see if she could find Toby, for he had not been out to play with her. Looking into the dining-room, she saw him there, eating luncheon with Mr. and Mrs. Carrenda. They were talking anxiously, and she was curious, and listened.

"I have it," said Mr. Carrenda suddenly. "Don't you remember those people – the Eeglines, or Eigleens – that came over to the hill near Mount Varcrobis where we lived before we came here? who wanted to know if we had seen a strange little girl, dressed all in ferns? She is the Eigleens' lost little girl."

Mrs. Carrenda looked puzzled, "They told us, you know, that they had given up all hope of having Ee – ee – serpip" (Toby started violently) "back again – "

"Oh yes, I remember now."

"– When Fleuriss came, and –"

"Oh yes, it all comes back to me now. They were making a great effort to find her and entice her back home by telling her about her baby sister."

"Yes."

"Why, father," said Toby, "Eepersip –" He suddenly saw her in his mind, kneeling in front of him, begging him not to tell – and he said no more. Nobody noticed his remark.

A moment Mrs. Carrenda gazed at her husband astounded. Then she said: "I believe it is so. Let us send word to them right off."

47

"No," said Mr. Carrenda, bluntly. "Supposing they came all the way down here. Supposing the plan failed. Mrs. Eigleen would only be unhappier than ever. We'll just have to let them alone for a while. Supposing *we* try it. Supposing it fails. Mrs. Eigleen will never know. Supposing it succeeds. They will be *much* happier, and we shall have made some staunch and grateful friends."

"Oh, let's try it!" agreed Mrs. Carrenda,

"I bet Eepersip – Ee-serpip, Eeserpip, Eepersip, Eeserpip, Eepersip – funny name! – I bet she'll go home fast when she finds out."

"Perhaps – but she is like a sea-nymph now. How strange it is! Well, it's worth trying, at any rate."

Eepersip had listened with growing amazement – fascinated, entranced. But when they paused in

their conversation, the charm was broken that had held her there. She sped away into the woods. She came to a place that she knew well, a glade surrounded by ferns and a few wild-rose-bushes now in bloom.

She had a little sister! – it was too much. And that little sister haunted her dreams and her imagination, making everything seem less joyful than before. She felt a strange longing – the longing to see her. She might be several years old now. Eepersip had forgotten what a "year" meant, but she had a vague feeling that Fleuriss had been living some time already. Why had no one told her? She felt a sort of angry resentment, but it cooled immediately when she remembered that her parents *had* been trying desperately to tell her. Yes, a plan was certainly shaping itself in Eepersip's mind – but not the plan of letting herself be caught, tamed, and carried home. No indeed. She dreamed of someday going home by stealth, seeing Fleuriss, and playing with her as she now played with Toby. She wondered silently if she would be anything like the fair-haired little boy. She wondered whether Fleuriss, too, would play with her secretly. If Fleuriss were like Toby, how wonderful it would be!

But the problem of getting back home to see her did not appear so serious to her now while she had Toby to play with.

*****

She continued her beloved explorations, discovering islands, beaches, peninsulas, and rocks out of sight of land, which she charted dawn in her mind, so that she could almost always find them.

One day Toby came to her and told her that they were going off on a tramp, rowing over across the bay to the woods near a little cottage that Mr. Carrenda knew about. They had always been interested in the cottage; they wanted to see who was living there. And they had heard about some beautiful hills behind it, which Mr. Carrenda wanted very much to see. And if it was pleasant they were going to start the next day. Eepersip was curious. She wondered if it could possibly be *her* cottage and *her* hills – the cottage she had discovered, and the hills that she had climbed about in. She decided to follow and see where it was that the Carrenda's were going.

When the boat started she let it get same way off, then she plunged into the sea and followed it. The waves came up behind, and she gained fast, but when she got dangerously near she stopped for a while, waiting for the boat to get farther off. They landed just where she thought they might – by the little cottage.

Near it they set up their tent, and soon they were exploring the peninsula. They climbed the beautiful hill which Eepersip had climbed. Once they saw her as she darted behind a tree, and wondered how she had got there so quickly. And they fell to talking about her again. She heard them talking over their plan of capturing her, telling her about Fleuriss, and, when she had been smoothed down a bit, letting her go back to the Eigleens to make them happy. If only they could have foreseen!

They tried only once, and never had the chance again. It was a golden day in October. Eepersip was sitting on a rock repairing some tears in her sea-weed dress. The waves were high, and every once in a while a little spray would splash up on to the rock where she was sitting. Mr. Carrenda discovered her sitting there, and, tiptoeing forward, he caught her by the shoulders. She gnashed her little white teeth at him and struggled to get away, but he held her fast, and was about to pick her up in his arms. She shouted: "O waves, help me!" And, magically, a great wave rushed up, whirled itself into the air, and broke in Mr. Carrenda's face. He dropped her, and with a lightning maneuver she dived down from the rock into the sea, and was far out before he recovered from the surprise. After this she remained far from the cottage and made her home on a deserted island.

This island was a lovely place. It had a beach of fine sand on one side and was entirely surrounded with rocks on the other sides – rocks and, in places, even high cliffs. There was a grove of yellow pines there, where Eepersip danced when she wished to turn nymph again. There was a spring of fresh water on a small hill behind the grove. The hill was still covered with blueberries and raspberries; also there was a multitude of the plants with the sweet white roots that Eepersip was so fond of. There were asters, too, and Eepersip wove them in with her ferns or sea-weed, and crowned herself with them. Very happy to find not a single house on the island, she lived there for a long time, glad also to be able to have both the sea and the woods, to which she still instinctively returned occasionally. The period through which she stayed on this uninhabited island was one of the happiest stretches of her life by the sea.

But, now that she was alone again, Eepersip was filled once more with longing to see the little sister – to know her, love her, play with her, teach her to leap and dance and swim; filled with curiosities about what was going on at the home which she had been away from for so long. And these emotions grew and grew until they became a firm resolution. She struggled a while to prevent herself from thinking she had made a mistake in running away, and, thinking it all over, said that she had not, even if she did miss such exciting things as little sisters.

The plan of seeing Fleuriss had become more and more developed, now that she saw little of the boy and had more time to think about it. (It was only once in a while that she swam to the mainland to play with him.) Her idea had changed a great deal: it now was to take Fleuriss away to live with her. She wondered whether she could ever get her over those awful crags, through that shadowy forest, to the sea; whether she could make her comfortable living the wild life. Here was a difficult situation, for Eepersip was sure that so young a child could never endure the hardships of the life she lived – at least, until she was used to it.

This problem troubled her mind for days. Then, suddenly, as she was gazing over the restless, murmuring sea, she had a great inspiration. "Oh! beautiful!" she exclaimed in her delight. The vision of the little brown cottage in the grove of white pines had come back to her – the whole thing, how she had been borne to it on her raft by those friendly yet terrible waves. And now she had a use for it! It seemed strange, when she hated houses so. But, then, no one need know. She would go at once and make sure whether the Carrendas had gone from their camp, then fix up the cottage and discover all its secrets. *Then* she could go and take Fleuriss away.

So one cold day she swam – back to the cottage. The Carrendas' tent was gone; everything was as it had been before. But this time it did not appear hateful. She opened the door and went into the pleasant little living-room with the fireplace. Then she investigated the whole house thoroughly. She found a room with glass cupboards on the walls, filled with a marvelous collection of all kinds of sea-weeds, shells, and corals (how Fleuriss would enjoy them! she thought); and there was a tiny kitchen. There was one small attic room, with a ladder going up to it through a trap-door, and in it was a soft little bed with warm blankets, and a fireplace. Above the bed were three casement windows, and Eepersip liked to think how it would delight Fleuriss to see the stars out these. When she went to the second floor she came to a snug alcove with glass doors opening on to a porch, free to the wind and sun, overlooking the sea; and two sunny bedrooms.

But just as she was preparing to start after Fleuriss, her reason again detained her. Fleuriss of course could not begin her wild life in the winter: she must have a summer of it first, to see what it was like. So Eepersip waited patiently till spring. During the winter she lived in a great pasture on a hill behind the cottage.

*****

The spring came round incredibly soon, and again Eepersip prepared to start.

The night before she went a great black cloud came up from the west, and soon a gale was raging. The waves mounted higher than any Eepersip had ever seen before, topped with flying snow-white spray. They leaped the highest cliffs, thundered on the wet rocks, and then retreated, swashing down through the cracks with a strange hollow sound and sweeping the sea-weeds wildly up and down. The wind sounded as on a mountain-top, a curious mixture of high-pitched whistling and bass droning. Occasionally it would rise into a terrific scream, making the waves rage with the uncanny storm-green. At the crisis of the storm Eepersip, who had been standing on the beach watching, her curls flying, her ferns fluttering and often tearing loose, flung herself into the storm from a high rock, and was swept about like a tiny insect, disappearing under a wave, bobbing up to take a breath just as the next breaker washed over her. She had a glorious time out in the waves and the spray. The sea-gulls shrieked; sometimes they struck at a fish, and appeared all covered with spray and shaking the drops from their wings – strong narrow wings that beat down the air as the birds rose again, to hover and swoop and plunge. These marvelous birds being blown wildly in the gale reminded Eepersip of the swallows, as they were tossed about by the high pasture winds – the swallows she had loved so when she lived on the meadow.

Slowly the wind abated its fury, and Eepersip, covered with water-drops and spray like a silver fish or a sea-gull, swam to the shore bubbling with happiness. With the water still standing on her hair, she sang a sea-song on the beach, accompanied by the rocking waves, now calmed down, and by the screaming and wildly circling gulls.

It was a wonderful night afterwards, for soon the sea was entirely calm, and the moon and the stars came out, reflecting themselves in trembling silver. Eepersip was up all that night, dancing, singing, swimming and diving in the glorious moonlight. And then she remembered – to-morrow! and went up on the hill to say good-bye to the meadow, the pastured hill, and the quiet, mossy pool that she had loved so.

Up on the hills she saw the sun rise. First the dark blue sky turned grey, and then a pearly streak came on the horizon as the first ray of the sun appeared; then it turned to the most heavenly shade of pink and deep rose, and then into the blue of one of the most gorgeous days Eepersip had ever seen. She gazed and gazed at the dawn until it grew pale and buttercup yellow, and finally turned to blue. The sun made a mass of gold sun-sparkles on the sea, and they blended together from the high hill and formed a solid splotch of gold, separating at the edges into individual sparkles. It was a windy day, but the wind was warm, and at first the sea was only rippling gently and smiling.

Then Eepersip remembered her little sister Fleuriss, and she wished her already there to share that beautiful, beautiful day. And off at one end of the beach she found, to her delight, a little green boat with two oars, which had been washed in by the storm. Now she had everything she needed, for the clumsy raft was difficult to manage in the wind, and she might even be blown so far off that she could never find the cottage again. Now, however, all was ready.

And so she made her way home, beginning in the boat, and rowing to where she had first entered the sea; then past the great precipices over which she had so laboriously clambered as she went to the sea, over hills, down into valleys, crossing, rivers, and tearing her way through forests, until at last, to her delight, she arrived at the beautiful meadow where she had spent her first years of wildness with Chippy, Snowflake, and the deer.

The deer did not remember Eepersip; that was one thing which distressed her. But a little fawn came cautiously and sniffed at her, obviously wishing he dared to approach and eat the ferns of her dress. She did not see Chippy anywhere.

She was soon at her own house, spying around, and looking in windows. All she could think of was Fleuriss, her little sister.

CHAPTER III

THE MOUNTAINS

The droning wind Entwined about the peaks
A golden trail of music....
Far off, the snow-topped mountains
Were sea-waves Capped with foam.

EEPERSIP HAD BEGUN TO WONDER whether it would be so easy to take Fleuriss away. She might consent to play, like Toby; but to run away, like Eepersip? – it was a great problem. Eepersip must use some other means than simply appearing and asking her sister to go with her. Perhaps she could entice her on with the assurance that there was something wonderful waiting. Or maybe she could show Fleuriss wonder after wonder – point out the beautiful sea from far away, then lead her on to the little cottage which she had prepared. And if Fleuriss was cold, or hungry, what should she do then? Perhaps she would not like roots to eat. Then, suddenly, an idea: she would dress herself up in wonderful flowers interwoven with the ferns, she would lure butterflies about her wreaths, she would bear armfuls of roses and apple- blossoms and lilacs and scatter them over Fleuriss, she would make her a fern dress, and, thus fascinating her, draw her away.

Eepersip wondered where she could sleep, near the house, and yet concealed. She thought of returning to the meadow, but that would be too far for convenient communication with Fleuriss. And then she saw a lilac-bush on the eastern side of the cottage – a great tall lilac-bush, thick and with great branches. It looked as though she could go into it. And when she tried, she found, to her great delight, that she could squeeze in, curl up in comfort, and be absolutely invisible from the outside.

Then she began to make her fairy array, weaving more ferns into her skirt, and more and more, until it was thick and flouncy – maiden-hair ferns and Christmas ferns, evergreen ferns and hay-scented ferns. She tucked flowers all over her dress – late daffodils, cosmos, wild geraniums, primroses. She made a girdle of yellow daisies, a crown of golden buttercups; she plucked a bunch of roses, lilacs, and ferns, binding them with daisies woven together. A great bouquet of violets decorated her dress – violets and little white Pyrolas. With a huge hollyhock for her wand and her arms full of lilacs and roses, she danced in the woods, thinking how her little sister would wonder – and follow.

That evening early she climbed an oak which was beside the window of her former room, and peeped in. The moonlight shone on the face of a child lying in a little wooden crib. She had fluffy black curls and bright, snapping black eyes, and she was watching delightedly the shadows of the branches on her wall and softly humming.

"Oh," breathed Eepersip, "the little sister. I want her, I want her!" Entranced, Eepersip watched, sitting in a crotch just outside the window – watched her as she lay there, tracing with her finger the curving patterns on her wall-paper; as she played with her hands in the moonlight and the waving shadows on her wall. And after a while the humming died away, the finger ceased to stroke the wall, her eyes closed, and in a moment she was gently sleeping. Before Eepersip went down she left a fair sprig of apple-blossoms on Fleuriss's bed – apple-blossoms that, with difficulty, she had brought up the tree.

When she went back to her lilac-bush she imagined Fleuriss's surprise, when she should wake, to see them on her bed; imagined Fleuriss following her, all fascinated by butterflies and sweet flowers; imagined her little sister climbing mountains with her, eating berries and roots, swimming and diving and dancing; and – her thoughts began to grow more and more fantastic – the smell of lilacs intoxicated her – and she went to sleep.

*****

In the morning she climbed the tree again. Fleuriss was just waking. Her eyes were turned toward the lovely oak-tree, watching the sunlight playing on the emerald leaves. She caught a glimpse of Eepersip as she vanished around the trunk.

"Oh, Mother," she called softly, "I saw a nymph! She smiled at me, and went away."

"Hush, child," said Mrs. Eigleen, coming upstairs and stroking gently the silky black hair. "You were only dreaming."

"No, Mother," returned the child, "I was awake. I *saw* a nymph, really." Mrs. Eigleen only smiled.

And then Fleuriss saw the flowers. "O Mother," she cried, "did you bring those to me?" Mrs.

Eigleen was wonderstruck.

"Why, no!" she answered.

"Maybe that nymph left them here."

Mrs. Eigleen was astounded enough not to contradict her. "Perhaps," she said.

Eepersip descended again and ran off to her safe hiding-place in the lilac-bush. "She is so, so lovely!" she thought. "I want her more and more."

In a short time little Fleuriss appeared with Mrs. Eigleen. "Fleuriss," said her mother, "you may play here in the garden, but don't go outside it, and don't climb the trees."

"All right, Mother."

"And don't run off and worry me as you did once before." She had *not* forgotten Eepersip.

Perhaps she scented something mysterious in the air. Those flowers troubled her. "No, I won't."

Mrs. Eigleen went in, and Fleuriss began to run about and play. Then Eepersip stepped out from under the bush, and the lovely butterflies, lured by her flowers, fluttered and hovered around her.

"Oh," said Fleuriss, "goodness, how you frightened me. Sit down on the grass, and talk with me.

And *how* do you get those butterflies? They always fly away from me."

"Listen, Fleuriss," said Eepersip. "I am Eepersip, who ran away. The butterflies and birds all love me and come to me in great flocks when I call them. And I want you. I want to take you with me to live wild, and eat leaves and berries with the birds – sweet red berries. And if you come the butterflies will gather around you, too. They will not any other way. And look at all my flowers! Butterflies love my flowers."

"Oh, did *you* bring me those *bee-yoo-ti-ful* flowers?" "Yes, I did. Come!"

"Oh," answered Fleuriss, "and wouldn't it be funny if Mother came out and found me not here!" "And think – the birds, the butterflies, the flowers! Look, I'd dress you like this, with ferns and

flowers and butterflies. And what fun we could have! We would dance and sing and chase each other amongst the fluttering leaves:"

"Oh, I could never catch you."

"No, but I could catch you, and that would be as much fun."

"But Mother doesn't like me to eat leaves, and berries all the time make one sick."

"But we would not have berries all the time. We would dig up sweet white roots and wash them clean; and *m-m!* they are good, little sister Fleuriss. We would have honey. The bees gather honey from the flowers, which they would share with us."

"Bees sting," said Fleuriss, shrinking away; "they sting, and they hurt, Eepersip."

"Oh, but the bees love us all so they don't sting us," answered Eepersip. "It's only the people that try to hurt them that they sting. We wouldn't hurt them."

"Oh, *Eepersip!* the leaves and butterflies, and – and honey – *m-m!* But I oughtn't, really," she said, backing off toward the house.

"Oh, come," said Eepersip, "come, don't go away. Your Mother wouldn't care; she would love to see how happy you were. *Please* come." And Eepersip's hands went out in supplication, scattering over Fleuriss wreaths of flowers, sprays of berries, crimson, gold, frosty white.

"Oh, how beautiful!" exclaimed the little girl. But when she looked up, Eepersip had vanished.

*****

Suddenly the door opened and Mrs. Eigleen stepped out. Eepersip had darted under the welcome branches of an apple-tree, whose thick blossoms kept her from sight.

"How sweet it smells!" said Mrs. Eigleen – "just as if a fairy had been here. Where

57

did those flowers come from, Fleuriss?"

"Oh," answered Fleuriss, "I saw the most beautiful girl. She brought me flowers and called me 'little *sister*' and wanted me to go away with her!"

Pale and weak from fright, Mrs. Eigleen took Fleuriss by the hand and dragged her roughly into the house.

Eepersip sat down under the apple-tree in ecstasy. "I saw her," she said softly, "I saw her and talked to her, and – oh, how dear she is! But I *do* wish she hadn't told about me." She waited there, and in a short time Fleuriss appeared again, running.

"Eepersip, Eepersip," she cried, "where are you?"

In a moment Eepersip had her arms around her waist, kissing her and hugging her. "Are you coming?" she asked; "have you decided to come, Fleuriss?"

"Y-y-es," said Fleuriss, "I really have, Eepersip. I thought all dinner time, and couldn't eat, I was so 'xcited! But we must go quickly now, or they will run after us."

So they ran quickly into the woods – ran amid the trees and flowers until they were far from the house. Eepersip showed her little sister how to dance, and they danced together. She also showed her how to leap and run fast, and Fleuriss was delighted. When they grew tired, they sat down together and made fern dresses and flower wreaths. Fleuriss followed Eepersip's example, casting aside her dress, shoes, and stockings.

"Oh, how 'licious the grass feels on my bare toes!" she said, "and the soft moss. Eepersip, I feel just like a nymph." (A slight pause.) "When I saw the flowers I said: 'Mother, I think a *nymph* left them there,' and she said: 'Oh, no, there aren't any nymphs. You're only dreaming!' Are there nymphs, Eepersip?"

"Oh, yes, Fleuriss, and if we dance and run and dress just like them, we'll pretend *we're* nymphs, too."

"But why can't we see them, Eepersip?"

"Oh, we can, if we look very hard. They're all around in the trees, the flowers, and the woods.
Sometimes we can't see them, and they turn into butterflies so we can. I can see them."

"Well, sometimes," said Fleuriss thoughtfully, "it seems as if they were everywhere – when it's windy, you know, and sunny, and there are shadows. In my garden it's so beautiful I think there must be nymphs. I can *feel* them, not exactly see."

There was a pause.

Then – "Where we going now, Eepersip?" for Eepersip was gradually working off to a hill which was a peak of Mount Varcrobis, north of Eiki-ennern Peak.

"Fleuriss," said Eepersip, with a strange emotion in her voice, "have you ever seen the sea?"

"No, but I heard Mother talking about it once. She said maybe you had gone down there; and she told me it was lots of blue water, and there were boats there. Did you really go there?"

"Yes; it's *so* beautiful, Fleuriss. The sun makes the waves sparkle like gold, and the great white gulls with their long, narrow wings go gliding, circling over the water, sometimes plunging down and catching fish underneath. And there is white sand there, soft sand, and shells and pretty pebbles, and little fishes swimming. And when it's windy the waves come dashing up on the rocks, flinging spray high in the air. And there is sea-weed, too, Fleuriss, green sea-weed that goes floating up and down as the waves stir it. And corals, too. Oh, my little sister, it's so, so beautiful. I would show you how to leap into it from the rocks, and how to swim – to be a mermaid and play with the gulls and the fishes, dressed all in sea- weeds!"

"Oh, Eepersip! Let's go *now!*"

"And I have a little cottage down there for you to live in – a pretty little cottage just like your home."

"Oh, how nice!"

"And we shall go riding up and down on the great waves, Fleuriss, while the sea-gulls scream over our heads. We shall go 'way out of sight of land and find islands and rocks out there. And the waves are tremendous when it's windy – very windy,"

"Fleuriss!" And Eepersip caught her little sister in her arms – glad that she had succeeded in entrancing her with the sea.

"But, Eepersip," said Fleuriss, doubtfully, "where *are* we going now?"

"I thought, Fleuriss, that we'd go to that great hill over there – do you see?" "Yes."

"Go over there so that you can see from 'way off how beautiful it is." "Oh yes; I'm crazy to see it!"

Eepersip saw that this hill was wooded on one side, but on the far side it was like a pasture – she could see sunlight glinting on it. On they went, often stopping to pick flowers, to dig up roots, or to refresh themselves at some little tinkling brook or mossy spring. Once as they were pushing through a fence of low beech-branches they came to a spring all surrounded with green moss – oh! so soft. There were ferns nodding beside it, and one or two, strange pink orchids gazed at themselves admiringly in its surface. At the bottom were white stones. A cool, green frog plopped into it as they arrived. And Fleuriss was fascinated. She sat there for a long time, watching him reappear for air, then bob down again when he saw that they were still watching him.

Again they came into a great meadow dotted with flowers. Butterflies with soft wings stroked Eepersip's cheeks caressingly. Fleuriss danced through the flowers, looking, as Eepersip thought, like a little butterfly herself. The sky was a heavenly deep blue – a rich deep blue, yet filled and sparkling with all the gold of the sun and all the coolth of snow. She could see for miles into it, as if it had suddenly come nearer than usual. She reached up and could almost see her fingers touching it. What a strange sensation!

But Fleuriss had a stranger one. As Eepersip danced along, it seemed as though her feet barely touched the ground. The flowers and grasses swayed gently beneath her, but they were not crushed. And Fleuriss felt a bit of dread coming into her mind – dread of living and staying with this strange sister.

What if she should grow tired of Fleuriss and run off? Suppose she should change into a tree – a leaf – a sprite? But Fleuriss fought with this feeling – because she wanted to live by the ocean, and to do the things that Eepersip had promised.

*****

After a while they came to the foot of the great hill. They slept down there, near a tiny lakelet, in the soft grass and among the flowers, with the tinkle, tinkle of a little brook in their ears all night. The next morning they climbed the hill together, and it was very steep and rocky. Fleuriss had to be helped often, and grew tired before she reached the top. But Eepersip lured her on by the promise of seeing the ocean, and they struggled painfully up.

The sea stretched away to the horizon, blue and sparkling as it met the sky. Fleuriss was spellbound.

"Eepersip, is that the sea?" she asked. "Yes, Fleuriss – the sea, the sea!"

Off to the north was a range of high blue-green hills, and off beyond them higher ones, and higher – billowing mountains – and beyond them was a range of snowy peaks, rising, sharply outlined, into the blue. The lakelet where they had slept was like an opal set with dark green pines. But those mountains – ! never before had Eepersip seen anything like them. The sea was not nearly so beautiful. And again she felt that longing which she had felt when she saw the sea – but a more passionate longing.

And Fleuriss? How could she climb those great peaks – she, who had had great difficulty even with the little hill? Well, Fleuriss could grow more used to such things, and then they would go together. But Fleuriss – Fleuriss barefoot, dressed in ferns – on those snowy summits! No, it would be impossible for years and years. She would have to wait – or else go alone.

But the hill had other things than just the view. For there were the loveliest little winding lanes, and bright open places, and close spots where they could hardly push through the bushes; great patches of delicious soft grass, then again enormous smooth-topped rocks from where they had first found the long- sought vision of the sea. Such feasts as Nature laid before them! There were great beds of the most delicious wild strawberries, and nobody to share them with but the birds. And they and the birds gobbled them; and it seemed as if the more they ate the more there were to eat; they ripened all the time. And in this marvelous place there were such contrasts! They could have anything they wanted there. There were places where the sun always struck brilliantly, and cool, shady ones for the hot days – places where not much sun ever came. There was the loveliest of soft grass, and then again nothing but brambles and heaps of pointed rocks. There were lanes leading through the woods occasionally, and there were places where no one would ever suspect that there was any such thing as a lane. There were little fairy glades where they could dance together – glades bordered with ferns and carpeted with moss.

Fleuriss and Eepersip lived there enchanted day after day, and although they often saw the sea, they did not wish to leave the hill. Fleuriss spoke about it several times, but Eepersip would hurriedly change the subject. That range of blue hills seemed to be calling her – she would forget the sea for a while, until the next year. After they had stayed where they were for some time, they would go on and on to the blue hills, and perhaps explore the great snowy mountains beyond. She could manage with Fleuriss somehow.

One day they went exploring farther than ever toward the east. They followed a narrow path, winding, winding through the bushes. And then it curved around toward the north-east and led through low laurel-trees, and here Eepersip stopped to make for Fleuriss a crown of the blossoms. And again the path turned and came on to a broader gravel road all bordered with gorgeous roses of red and white, and Fleuriss was very much surprised at their magnificent beauty. But Eepersip was distressed. So they had come to a place where there were roads, houses, and people! But as yet they had seen no house. Eepersip hoped that there would be none, for she was as entranced as Fleuriss with the beauty of it all. And then they switched off on another little path, leading southeast on to a wide lawn all bordered with marvelous roses. Here they danced together a long time. Next they turned into another graveled path which led eastward, through clumps of roses and laurel, downhill and uphill, for a long way; and then they saw a garden brilliant with color. Fleuriss was dazed, there were so many flowering bushes – rhododendron, laurel, honeysuckle, azalea, quince; and fire-blossom. Hummingbirds, bright emerald and ruby with moonlight wings, were darting and sparkling about, sipping honey, resting and quivering on the air.

But soon after they had discovered the garden, Eepersip said that she was going on a short journey, coming back in two or three days. "Will you be all right here alone, little sister?" she said anxiously.

"Oh yes, Eepersip, and I'm going to find lots of things to show you when you come back. But where are you going?"

"I'm going – going – to a beautiful place – and take you there sometime." "Oh – I see. Can't I go now?"

"No – because – it would be too hard now. Wait till I go and find the easiest way for you." "All right – good-bye!"

And, with a rustle of ferns, Eepersip vanished around a great rhododendron-bush.

*****

Fleuriss continued her explorations alone. She saw a gorgeous butterfly come sailing toward her, of yellow streaked with black. Others followed, and they covered her with soft wing-caresses, crowning her head with their wings. Fleuriss thought (as Eepersip had told her) that they were the fairies turning themselves into butterflies so that she could see them.

Not a mouse stirred when she wormed her way through the bushes, taking care not to step on leaves or dry twigs so as to make a noise. And then the sun started to set and turned the whole sky golden and rose. Fleuriss crept in among a vine with golden flowers (there was no rich purple fruit yet, only the lovely flowers) and watched. And, each leaf was quivering, and on their smooth surfaces was represented another miniature sunset. How marvelous the rose and gold looked through the mass of trembling green leaves!

Then Fleuriss squeezed her way out of the bush and began to explore again. Pushing northward in the dim, rosy light, she came to a smooth lawn of pale green moss. On the other side was a stretch of woods, then another lawn, of grass this time and smaller; and then there was a great row of massive pines and beyond them an opaline lake. And still the sun went down, and the mass of color became smaller and brighter, and Fleuriss, who had never seen so much beauty in her little life, gazed and gazed. The color faded slowly; slowly, as she watched, until only a deep flush was left, and it was then that Fleuriss thought she was in the heart of a giant rose. And – inconceivable – she looked, and she *was*. She was sure of it. She could even see the great curling petals around her. Right at the sun was a burning spot. That was the pollen of the great flower. And this tiny fire burned and burned until only one bright red spark was left. Then it too went out, and after it all the rose color faded away.

Then Fleuriss turned to the lake, which also had held in its bright blue surface an image of the sunset. The sky was deep blue now. The pines looked even darker against it, and in the lake Fleuriss could see the reflection of the crescent moon setting. And then she ran down by the side of the lake, and very dark and strange it looked in the evening. Dipping her little hands into the clear, crystal water, she drank, for she was thirsty. But she was too tired to appreciate any more beauty just then, and so she crept back to her little nest of flowers to go to sleep. Then she heard a gurgle of sweet silvery music, and she listened spellbound, entranced. But it was no wicked witch, seeking to entice her by spells: it was the solitary wood-thrush, that superb singer of the dusk. And then Fleuriss dropped off to sleep.

The next morning dawned fair, and she rose bewitched with what she had been through. The sunset and the silvery notes of the thrush all came back to her. She went down by the lake. It was very different now. Its blue was sparkling with the rays of the sun, whereas before it had looked very solitary – an icy cold blue. There was no beach

– just a grassy bank – and in the shallow water she saw some little silvery fishes swimming and playing in shoals. And she watched them in their happy play for a long time, fascinated by the way they raced after each other around the shining stones and pebbles. Because they were so bright and gleaming, poor little Fleuriss thought that they were some rare and unheard-of fish, little dreaming that they were just common minnows.

Eepersip came back that day in a strange way. Fleuriss was looking down on the meadowy side of the hill, where the long green grass waved in the wind and butterflies were fluttering. And as she looked, suddenly – there was Eepersip standing in front of her. She had come from nowhere – she was just there without coming at all. Fleuriss was appalled. She remembered that strange dancing – was her sister about to melt into the air? Fleuriss stood stock-still.

Finally she raised her head and said, at first faintly, but with growing enthusiasm: "Oh, Eepersip, last night there was a great rose, and I was inside it – and I found a beautiful lake with fishes in it – oh wonderful fishes of silver – and the beautiful birdie sang me to sleep in the flowers." And then, her voice sounding strangely timid: "O Eepersip – I want – *Mother* – to see it – so beautiful. I love – it here, but – I know Mother – would like to see it, too. And I guess I can't get along without her. I guess I can't, Eepersip."

Eepersip was broken-hearted. "But, Fleuriss," she said – and Fleuriss shuddered a very little as Eepersip took her hand – "Fleuriss, if your mother came she would take you back home, and you would not be here anymore. If she would come to see it, all right, but she would not – and so, you would not see it either. Come on, show me the lake you found."

Fleuriss was happy in a flash. Laughing and dancing, she took her sister down to the lake and showed her the wondrous fishes. They went in bathing together, and Eepersip showed Fleuriss how to swim, as she had shown Toby. Fleuriss was wild with joy. Then they splashed each other and played tag in the water. Eepersip puzzled Fleuriss by swimming under water, and Fleuriss would scream with delight when she came up in a totally unexpected place. This new pastime kept them happy for several days.

But again Fleuriss began to grow miserable – and homesick.

*****

And again Eepersip resisted this feeling for a long time – two or three weeks of misery. But at the end of that time she began to think.

To begin with, she thought about where she had been on that little expedition of hers. She had been up toward those blue hills to see from nearer the snowy mountains. She had loved them more and wanted more than ever to go to them. She asked Fleuriss if she would not like to climb the high peaks with her. But Fleuriss replied, almost snappishly: "You know what I want, Eepersip."

Of course this misery weighed down Eepersip's mind frightfully; she was very uncomfortable.

And then she began to think that after all she would want to be alone when she went amongst the mountains; Fleuriss would be all right if she were happy, perhaps, but a miserable companion would be unendurable. Perhaps she had made a mistake in taking Fleuriss away. Maybe it was true that they had to go in different directions – that she herself could not live at home, and that her little sister could not live elsewhere. And even in Eepersip's untamed heart there was a bit of pity. And she found that that pity kept growing. How badly the Eigleens must feel, after all! Once she smothered it with the thought, "No, she will be happy if she stays long enough, and they will forget her." But it only began to grow again.

Up to this unhappy time Fleuriss's flowers had not withered or drooped: in this they were like those of Eepersip. But now Eepersip noticed that for some peculiar reason hers only stayed fresh and sweet. And then she thought again about the mountains and about those poor wasted flowers, and the pity grew and grew. And one happy, happy day for Fleuriss, Eepersip led her safely home again.

"Good-bye, Fleuriss," she said. "I'm sorry you wouldn't stay with me."

"Yes, I know, Eepersip, but I just couldn't. Why don't you come home? – you've been away so long – and Mother cries for you still. Please come."

"Oh, Fleuriss, I *couldn't*. If I were to go back home now, I should just die – even with you." "Good-bye, then. Sometime I'm going to take Mother to see that beautiful hill."

"But not for a long time?" "As soon as I can." "Don't."

"Why?"

"You know. Please don't."

"Well, I'm not sure. I'm going to – pretty soon. Good-bye, Eepersip – Aren't you ever coming home?"

"Oh, Fleuriss, no!" "I wish you would." "But I can't."

"Won't you let me take Mother and Daddy to live over there?" "Well, after a while – if you want to. I shan't be there."

"Why, where are you going?"

"I'm going to the beautiful, beautiful white mountains. And then maybe the sea again, Fleuriss–the sea."

"Oh!"

"Coming?"

"NO! I'll ask Mother to take me to the sea. She will." "Then – good-bye!"

And she decked Fleuriss's fern dress with beautiful flowers – a crown of them and a girdle. A sweet wind arose, carrying the scent of Eepersip's flowers to Fleuriss. A few butterflies were blown over to her. Eepersip stood on her tiptoes an instant: then, quick as a flash, she whirled about and bounded off, free – relieved of a gigantic burden.

*****

She went up to the lovely hill and stayed there a few days, amid the dancing butterflies and the gorgeous roses. At the lake she would dream hour after hour and watch the little jeweled minnows playing about the white stones and shining pebbles. In the evening she crept into a great bed of thick vines with flowers of white and gold, and listened to the lapping of the waves and watched the twinkling fireflies. They were her favorites, those poor ignorant little insects. She loved them as well as the delicate, gauzy butterflies, the sweeping swallows with their slim white wings, or the great gold-and-black bees. She adored them all, but the tiny blue-black fireflies, with thin gauze wings and the spot of phosphorescence showing now and then, were perhaps the loveliest of all. How she liked to see them playing about at dusk, sparkling and gleaming – little stars of the trees, in golden waves across the sky.

Sometimes, when they began to come out, she would go forth and dance and skip with myriads of them clustered in her hair. Around each invisible fern and blossom in her dress would gather a row of the little insects, until finally one could have seen her entire form bordered with fireflies. And besides these which alighted on her dress, thousands gathered swarming about her, so that her head was entirely hidden in a maze of gold.

Sometimes she would sleep at night and in the daytime play with the butterflies, birds, and bees.

But now she began to sleep more and more in the day and play about at night.

One cool morning Eepersip went down the lovely hill that she and Fleuriss had found. She walked down and then out toward the pastured side of the hill. Here she stayed for a long time. She lived in the golden smell of steeple-bush, and instead of the wild strawberries that she had had on the hill she found great crops of blueberries. And in this pasture she had a sample of a new food – checkerberries. To be sure, she had eaten the leaves often enough, but to see the waxen white berries was quite new. These also she tasted and found greatly to her liking. She would lie and eat hundreds of those white berries which tasted of the woods. They were almost as good as the blueberries.

Now this pasture formed a steep hill, and one delicious morning when a soft, warm wind was blowing rather strongly, Eepersip climbed to the top of it. And oh, what a sight met her dark brown eyes! Far and near, far and near rose mountains, mountains, mountains! Stretching away, fold after fold, layer after layer, rose marvelous blue peaks, with the dazzling light of the sun brightening the white granite at some of their tops. Peak after peak rose up around her, lake after lake stretched out in the dim blue distance, with the sun striking them until they were a mass of gold, like great precious stones in that setting of purple mountains. She could make out three or four farm-houses, but no villages. She stood there entranced, watching. Then down she dashed, through the tall grass sprinkled with buttercups and daisies. It seemed miles, but it also seemed no more than seconds. At last she found herself by the shore of a cobalt lake. It was almost perfectly round, with a group of tiny green islets sprinkled in it like a handful of emerald beads. No house could Eepersip see, for the lake was entirely surrounded with low green-blue hills. The shore was for the most part soft white sand, fine as pepper. With a cry of joy at the discovery of this beautiful little lake Eepersip dashed into it and swam in the cool of those waters from the mountains. And then she saw, playing up and down in the shallow water just off one of those many beaches, a shoal of slim fishes. They were all silver except one or two that were gold, and they had rather bulging red eyes.

For a long time Eepersip watched them. Then something caused her to look up. This something was the strange, shrill cry of a bird above her. She looked up suddenly and saw the bird. But she did not watch it: for the glint of something white – a strange whiteness which she had never seen before – caught her eye. She gazed long upon it, until, when her eyes became accustomed, she was able to make out the outline of a peak, going up sharp as a tooth, with bumps of smoother outline stretching away, away into the blue immensity of space on either side.

"Oh," said Eepersip, "a dream! Oh, what a beautiful dream! But – I feel so wide awake." She gazed and gazed, silent.

"Oh," she said again, after a while, "it cannot be a dream, it mustn't be a dream!" She gazed and gazed again.

"Oh," she repeated, "I must go – there at once! The snowy mountains!"

She plunged into the beautiful, icy lake and swam across it, with never a thought of the beauty in the green depths around her. Her eyes were fixed upon that one thing only. Soon she reached the opposite shore, consisting only of thick woods. Her heart – that heart beautiful, yet with a certain sense of childlikeness in it which had never left her – was mad for a glimpse of those mountains. It was then that she felt as if there were a great bird in her, pulling her, hauling her forward, regardless of the thorns and nettles which tore her delicate dress of ferns and blossoms. At last she got through the forest and found herself in an open meadow, with the wondrous mountain before her and warm rain falling gently. She saw a farmhouse, and as she went along the simple peasant farmer saw her and muttered to his wife: "Look there, Mary." Mary looked, and then she said: "Ay, God hath taken this child into his care – ignorance demands mercy."

A moment of intense thought. She gazed and gazed, bewitched. Then she gave, or tried to give, a little laugh. It did not sound. "Oh," she tried to say, "how *queer* I feel! I believe I never felt so queer." And indeed she did feel queer. For she felt the feeling of speaking to her heart. She was talking, it seemed to her, loudly, but when, even in the midst of her talk, she listened, nothing sounded.

After a few seconds, it seemed, she ran on, leaping through the wet. Raindrops gathered on the ferns and the flowers of her dress, outlining them with the pearly water. She looked like a rain-fairy. Hour after hour passed, and she went like the wind itself; yet she did not tire. At last she found herself near the foot of that wondrous mountain, shimmering with snow-fields, cold white against a deepening night sky.

That night a bird of modest wood-color, with speckled breast, sang of moonlight; and, rippling faintly, softly, came echoes from his silver-tongued mate. They sang, and they answered, and the moon- frost-tipped pines were quiet, and clouds floated near, snowy palaces of silence. Spellbound, Eepersip was borne away to fairy kingdoms where she danced – and where birds sang the only melody in the world.

*****

The next morning the sun came out and shone through every raindrop in splendid crimsons and purple-greens. Eepersip looked about her and discovered a little plant with a peculiar flower of white and crimson. She found that its leaves were quite delicious, unlike anything that she had had in the meadow or by the shore of the sea. They were green – a strange pale green, delicately outlined and veined in marble white and pale gold. Eepersip loved their pleasant flavor, but could not bear to touch them, they were so beautiful.

Then she looked up and beheld the strange rough outline of the mountain, and far in the distance, almost on the top, was a great snow-field, on which the sun shone directly, covering it incredibly with brilliant tints and shades of gold. And, oh, the bright green foliage, shining in the clear golden light!

"Fairyland!" whispered Eepersip. "I loved the meadow, I loved the sea more, but even before I am really *in* the mountains, I love them the best of all." Then, after a pause, she added: "That snowfield of gold, these heavenly little flowers – oh, such beauty!"

After a few more moments of breathless gazing, gazing upon everything, she started up the mountain. The first few hundred yards she followed a woods, over great boulders covered with dark green moss. Occasionally a little rushing brook trickled across her path. For quite a way Eepersip kept climbing over the huge boulders, and the path was very mossy. After a while it began to grow fainter and harder to follow, and at last it was shut off entirely by the thick bushes and trees which surrounded it. Here she sat down to rest and to think a while.

She looked about and came upon a bubbling spring, at which she drank. No water she had ever found was like this. It tasted of the strong, delicious mountain air. She drank deeply, and, when she had quenched her thirst, continued her way. Here flowers which made her think of foam at sea – white, star- like, with silver-tipped petals – twined themselves among the trees mingled with wild roses – dawn- flowers of deep pink or sun-bright yellow. Strange orchids grew about, many of them pure white and fringed like fluffy clouds. One had green blossoms with long whitish spurs – mystic flowers on tall spikes with two smooth leaves. Yellow lady-slippers made her think of butterflies with folded wings, or of the sun peeping, out from dark clouds. But the loveliest of all were pink orchids – hosts of them with more deeply tinted lips fringed like fairies' fingers; hosts of them on slender stems, each stem a dawn-sprite's wand.

"Like the dawn I saw once," she thought, "when snow-pink fringy flowers wreathed the sky. The sun was pleased and smiled. I danced for him, and the bobolinks and skylarks greeted him with song." There were tall flowers, too, pink silk beneath white tissue, with very dark and curious leaves up the stalks among the blossoms. Butterflies were playing like sunrays, winging softly from flower to flower. And as she went on she passed through forests of thick bushes and poisonous thorns, open pine- groves, and great pastures smelling of hay-scented ferns and budding steeple-bush.

All the time the path, or rather the easiest way through the thick bushes, had been fairly level, but now it began to shoot up steeply, and it was all Eepersip could do to keep herself from sliding back in an avalanche of pebbles and stones. A bit of tough scrambling followed, and at last she broke out on a comparatively level piece of ground, on one side of which was a deep ravine in which she heard a brook rushing and rippling. On the other side of the ravine was a peak of the mountain, crowned with snow and with the sun flashing upon it.

Eepersip longed to see the brook, which, by the sound, she judged to be quite large. She was not actually afraid to go down over those steep walls of dirt and sand, but she *was* rather afraid that, once being down, she would not be able to get up again. So on she went, and it grew so steep that, even by digging her feet into every crevice and clutching the roots of the trees, which were getting much scarcer and more stunted, she could just manage to cling on.

But at last a change came. She stood on that high peak, on which there were only bare rocks and a little snow, no roots or plants. On either side it went down, down, and it was getting late in the afternoon. She could see nothing to do. Still the highest peak was many miles ahead, and she knew that she could not make it in the remaining daylight. So she climbed warily down into a little crevice, where a few ferns and luscious mountain blueberries managed to grow. She ate a supper of these and of another hardy little berry which she found; then slept in peace till daybreak, her tired mind dreaming of strange things – of deep palaces at the bottom of the sea and snow palaces at the tops of the mountains; of fairies, nymphs, and elves.

*****

In the morning she breakfasted on the mountain blueberries again, and found, much to her delight, that they quenched her thirst almost as well as water. After her juicy breakfast she went on down for about a mile; then up, up again on sheer walls of rock, where there was not a sign of a plant of any kind. After a stretch of difficult climbing snow again began to appear, as the slope became more level.

Eepersip went down through a snug hollow in the rocks, where it was, thick with small, scrubby trees and where very little snow had managed to penetrate the thick branches.

Oh, but it was cold up here on these tremendous heights; the wind was keen, and shrilly whistling. But, however cold, it was a mountain wind, an exhilarating mountain wind which made Eepersip leap into the air – leap and dance as on the meadow. Then, after she had rested a while under the welcome branches of the stunted firs and eaten tart mountain blueberries again, she went on, up out of the hollow and on to the solid rock covered with deep snow, into which she sank at every step. Another mile she trudged along, pulling herself through it. And still the mighty peak retreated before her, so that she could make no progress – or, at least, it seemed so. It seemed as far away and as faint in the snowy distance as from where she had been when the night had come on – a dreaming peak caressed with fingers of mist.

At last the ground went up abruptly again. However steep, Eepersip found it much easier, because there wasn't so much snow. It rose and rose, becoming more gradual, until she stood on another high peak, looking off over a tremendous range of mountains. Large flakes of snow were falling gently, so that she could not see much of these. She thought that she was now on the highest peak, and she sat down to wait for the snow to cease and give her a clear view. After a time it did; and then, and not until then, she saw another peak, the true summit of the mountain, going up, up, and up on the other side of a deep valley into which she would have to descend. After sucking a few handfuls of the pure mountain snow, she set off with a light heart and a happy spirit, her feet falling fast through the light drifts. After a while she got down into the valley; and here she came upon a brooklet full of icicles, winding through the long ravine and dashing over the green slimy rocks in great cascades of rattling icicles and foam: Eepersip drank deeply, and was refreshed.

71

Then, after resting a few moments, she went on, up that steep wall of snow and rock which would take her to the longed-for summit. Eepersip counted sixteen brooklets rushing down over it, carrying hundreds of icicles with their currents; foaming and dashing with spray and myriads of shiny iridescent bubbles.

Across brook after brook she went, watching the colors change in the dazzling snowflakes. The sun was shining brilliantly now, making everything unimaginably beautiful in magnificent shades of ruby, copper, silver-gold, emerald, and sapphire. Each snowflake seemed covered with an almost invisible layer of tiny sparkling gems. And once, when Eepersip sat down in a deep snow-bank to watch and to rest, the sun happened to strike directly on one of the many brooklets that went dashing down the mountain-side, making it a blinding ribbon of silver and gold. Occasionally Eepersip saw the blossoms of the beautiful talatuna, with ruby-red leaves and blossoms of pale green and changing white. She thought that the leaves were *all* red, but when the wind flipped one over she saw that their backs were moon-white, pale but glistening.

On she went, through the incredible beauty of the fairyland about her. "Oh," she murmured to herself, "how marvelous it is! Oh, fairies, fairies." She whirled happily around. She had felt a few delicate touches on her shoulders, and at once the air was a-flock with glistening snowflakes. Each fern in her dress was bordered with a row of the fairy things, and her autumn hair was crowned white.

After a while a slight breeze sprang up and the big flakes whirled faster. The breeze rose and rose until it was a strong, cold wind, and she could not see a foot before her. The only thing to do was to wait for clear weather. But in that she was disappointed, for it was growing darker and darker, and at last she realized that night was coming on. So she lay down and ate a supper of snow, as it fell and fell.

*****

All night the snow whirled and whirled, and in the morning Eepersip was completely buried. It was a long, hard task to find her way out, or rather to push her way out, for almost as fast as the snow fell it froze into ice, so that there was on top of Eepersip a thick layer of ice. But just before she decided to give up and wait for warmer weather, she broke through. Out into the bright sunlight she came; and lo and behold! all the ferns on her dress and the dainty blossoms, together with her hair, were covered with a layer of ice which shimmered and sparkled in the sun like jewels set in something brighter than the brightest gold.

But as soon as she came out into the sun the ice began to melt and run off in all directions, and as she skipped and jumped about she was almost hidden in the shower of water-drops which flew from her as she ran.

And how beautiful, how fairy-like, she was! Each fern was covered with a thin layer of the melting ice, and the crown of pink blossoms around her curly hair was frozen likewise, their fair color persisting through the ice. Once in a while, when the sun touched her, she was a blaze of color – of silver and gold, with here and there a splotch of brilliant red as the sun struck a red flower.

After she had found that there was nothing to be eaten except snow, she sucked a few handfuls, flavored with the petals of the flowers which she wore. Then she went on, through paradises of silver, gold, and red, through deep hollows of shining green. Everything was something besides white, and the world that was in Eepersip's range of vision was fairyland.

But, as she went on, clouds began to float in – little white clouds. They grew thicker and thicker, until, before she had come near the highest peak, there was nothing but pearly mist – scudding grey mist, curling into fantastic shapes as it rose. She could see nothing, and she sat down in the snow to wait. That night a gale came up, whistling and howling around the peaks, reminding Eepersip of that storm at sea. What an awesome sound it made! It sleeted, too, and when she awoke the next morning the snow was covered with a crust. The mist had partly cleared, and she pushed on again. She went through icy hollows and up on shimmering peaks, until, finally, she saw near her that long-sought summit, and, with a shout of joy, she dashed up. Fast she went, but when she really reached it at last, the mist had closed in again, the wind was up, and it was sleeting furiously. It was only through a break in the mist that she had made the summit at all.

*****

The next morning it was still misty, but not nearly so thick. There was a faint purple glow over on the eastern horizon where the sun was rising. Occasionally the mist would break open above, and she would see glimpses of blue sky – the deep deep blue of that day in the meadow with Fleuriss. And lying all around on the boulders were frost-feathers. When Eepersip first saw them she thought that she was dreaming. But no, they were really there, delicate ferns and feathers with scalloped edges – ferns and feathers of frost.

"Oh, mountain-fairies – fairies have left them here," she said quietly. Some were as long as her forearm, and others tiny – oh, so tiny; some were almost round like the inner feathers of a bird and others long and narrow like the outer plumes. Down in a hollow were some stunted firs laden with snow and covered with those fronds of ivory chiseled by wind-sprites, lovelier than anything Eepersip had ever seen, lovelier than anything ever made by Nature. No, Nature could never have carved them, Eepersip thought. The fairies – fairies!

Once she found a hollowed rock entirely lined with them, like a fairy's crystal palace with strange shadowy recesses. They crowded everywhere they could find room, and sometimes, when there was no other place, rippled on the snow. They overlapped on the rocks, and hung from windward crags, pointing into the wind. And behold! Eepersip's dress and her head were covered with small ones, like a diadem – a fairy crown and fairy ornaments. Moving gently, so as not to disturb them from where they rested, she wandered from one cluster to another, looking carefully at each one, noting each special pattern, each magic tracery. All day she followed the winding rabbit-trails amid the feathery firs. The sun, too, had been pushing out. Now the mist opened in one direction; and Eepersip caught a fleeting glimpse of snowy peaks; but it closed again. It opened a trifle longer in another direction, and Eepersip saw, 'way down below, first low blue-green foothills and lakes golden with the sun, then higher purple hills, melting into range after range of billowing mountains, and valley after valley filled with white clouds rapidly lifting. The mist shut in. Another direction opened in the same way, with hills fading into mountains; and far off on the horizon was another range of snow mountains, lying just under great white clouds. There were clouds hanging over the valleys too, and they cast strange shadows on the sunlit trees far below. When the mist shut in, the golden lakes seemed to stay the longest, and after the mountains had entirely disappeared they could be seen as if hanging in mid-air, limpid pools of gold. And more sides opened, and more, the waits growing shorter in between, until, on a gust of mountain wind, the last of the mist went scudding away, banished, and the sun broke out into the blue sky. The snow sparkled, the mountains sparkled, the lakes and rivers sparkled, the frost-feathers sparkled, the air itself sparkled. And the mountains of the range that Eepersip was in, crowned with snow, gleamed like gold.

Down on one side of the snowy peak dashed a great river, green and swirling, covered with clots of foam. Sometimes it would cascade over the rocks – throwing up a fountain of spray, and sometimes it would slip over a smooth slide, then, whirling round and round in a rock basin, thunder down another great cliff in a shower of bubbles, rattling icicles, and foam. It cut its way through a green hollow in the snow, and where it tunneled under the snow-banks it was overhung with long, gleaming icicles.

Eepersip danced in the snow, among the frost-feathers, all that day – danced like a mountain sprite, leaping high, then running gracefully in a shower of water-drops which flew from her as the frost- feathers melted in the warmth of the sunlight. She danced down to the river and played there a while – played with the white foam.

At sunset she was again at the peak of her mountain. The sky was flushed with magic; a great cloud in the west became brilliantly fringed with gold and red-gold, the east was all submerged in a lilac sea, and a delicate laciness of pink trailed across the zenith. Sunset fairies alighted on the snow-peaks: they were fiery for a moment, and all the great snow-fields were flaming. Then the color faded to pink on the summits. But in the sky Nature still flung about her colors wildly – fire was in the zenith, the long bank of clouds was vividly fringed with red-gold, and there to the south it changed to caverns of shadowed pink and strange violet. Seas and bays and cloud islands formed out of it – seas of a strange greenish rose. Then one thrill and flame of gold spread about the whole earth; the snow at her feet was shadowy gold, and a pathway of it danced upon the air 'way to the horizon. It played upon each frost- feather; the eastern mountains were flushed with this soft gold.

And then, dizzy with the color and the beauty, Eepersip fell asleep, her fingers clutching the rosy snow.

*****

The next morning the frost-feathers had almost disappeared underneath a new snowfall. The air was full of its fresh scent, as it came down gently in tremendous flakes. Here and there Eepersip saw one of the lovely blossoms of the talatuna, with those same ruby-red leaves. How beautiful they were, growing in great clusters, just peeping through the snow! Once in a while a pale cream-colored mountain moth would flit before her. Occasional gusts brought swarms of tiny bottle-green, white-winged snow-beetles, and the air was a-buzz with them. Sometimes a blue or white insect like a firefly would hover past, a strange red light gleaming about its transparent body.

On and on Eepersip explored, seeing nothing but the wonderland about her – the fairy palaces of snow, the fluttering, hovering insects, and the beautiful mountain flowers. Following the icy river down, she came sometimes to a great cascade of the green water – a cascade coming over one of those great cliffs, washing down the snow, throwing up fountains and clouds of spray in its furious descent.

Sometimes it cut under the banks, making a green cave hung with icicles gleaming strangely. One of these had been made when the river was in flood; now it was large enough for Eepersip to stand in, and, wading in water about up to her knees, she went back into its innermost recesses, where the roar of the stream was muffled. There were fish there – trout playing in the whirlpools and riding, swiftly with the current. She found some odd bright stones and gleaming pebbles in this mysterious place, silent save for the deadened rush of water.

Sometimes, again, the rushing brook took such a steep course that Eepersip was forced to make a detour into the woods for a little way, through clumps of the firs, now growing less stunted, but hung with icicles which clicked together in the wind, sounding to Eepersip like fairy castanets. Even at this high altitude, she saw occasionally a white pine, each cluster of pale green needles laden with snow – tufts of snow which seemed to make little faces peering out from the tree. Bursts of happiness would overwhelm her now and then, and she would leap high and dart like some frightened deer or mountain nymph.

Once she found beautiful little violet-shaped pink flowers with bowed heads and feathery leaves – snow-pinks blooming there, thrusting their buds from the snow itself. She tucked a spray of them into her dress of fluttering ferns.

And then she would return to the river and follow it again. When the moon came, dappling the foamy water with silver, she watched it as it dipped down its forehead in the stream and touched the treetops with magic. Then she would go on again through the moonlit night. Once she came to a place where the brook separated, and she had a difficulty choosing which branch to follow.

And when the russet dawn reappeared, tipping the mountains with apple-blossom and fire, she had followed it to its goal in the very meadow from where she had started – a pool hitherto unseen by her. About a hundred feet across it was, beached with clean white pebbles. In it bloomed water-lilies, fragrant and white, with centers of gold; strange red flowers, too, she saw on the bottom, growing between the pebbles. Dragonflies with crackling wings swept over it in circles. She saw, too, a shoal of tiny fishes of a brownish color, striped with yellow. They would suddenly dart forward as if something had frightened them, and then poise themselves stock-still, mimicking so many sticks in the shadows of the abundant lily-pads.

She was wading about in the pool when suddenly – where there had been ground for her foot to rest on, nothing was there. The bottom of the pool under her foot had slid forward and collapsed!

Suddenly "Clug-glug, clug-glug, chugarum, glug!" reached her, as a big bull-frog's nose appeared by the side of a lily-pad. A second later the frog climbed up on the lily-pad and stared at Eepersip with his goggly eyes. She burst out laughing, he looked so ridiculous staring at her like that.

She stayed in the meadow, playing gaily among the leaves and flowers. Butterflies of all the colors of the rainbow swept over it ill, great flocks. Flowers bloomed so thickly that there was hardly any grass – white ones with waxen petals, striped and bordered with heavy golden bands; red ones with centers of dark green-gold, great blossoms of pink and purple, whose petals fluttered about in the breeze like butterflies.

One morning, she was awakened early by "Peep, peep, twitter-itter-ee-e-e-e-e, twit chirup; twitter-ee-e-e, twit!" She looked up and saw a great flock of snow-white birds with long narrow wings. They were flying northward. The flock was much more gigantic than Eepersip had supposed, for it kept on until she began to think that it was going round and round. But no: after ten or fifteen minutes the sky cleared, and she heard faintly in the distance: "Twitter-itter-ee-e-e-e-e, *ee-e-per-s-sip!* e-e-p, e-p, chirup."

Day after day she danced here, playing, as on the first meadow, with the butterflies, flowers, and swallows. And now, as she danced, she seemed to float through the air, her feet almost motionless.

Sometimes she would leap high and come down – *float* down – quite slowly. She seemed to have no weight at all, and a breeze would almost lift her off the ground and hold her up in the air. Indeed, when she ran with the wind behind her she would be *blown* along – blown like a leaf just above the flowers.

*****

One day she was dancing there – dancing and leaping in the long grass, amid the blossoms; Butterflies drifted over the sunny field – butterflies of red and yellow, blue and green, black and white, orange and purple. How gracefully they flew; how delicately they alighted on the flowers; how fairy-like they were, hovering for an instant over some blossom, then dipping their wings and starting off again!

Eepersip felt as though – as though she were going to be one of them; as though she were so happy that she must fly about with them, sip the honey from the flowers with them.

As she was thinking happily she heard a few faint peeps, which became louder as she danced toward a certain part of the field. Then there was a desperate twitter right at her feet, and, looking down, she saw a yellow fledgling hopping towards her. She picked him up carefully and saw that he had broken his left wing. She worked a moment with her hands and pulled the bone into place. Then she made him a comfortable nest of grass and set out to see where he had come from. Looking up, she saw a nest from which a bird was peering about anxiously. Straightway she took the little one from the nest *she* had made, and climbed the tree with it to its own nest; upon which the mother-bird gave a twitter of joy.

After doing this Eepersip descended the tree and continued her happy dance with the butterflies until evening. Then they all found shelters under the leaves, and the stars came out, one by one. Presently Eepersip spied a flicker in the meadow – then another and still another, until the fireflies were out in full play. They gathered around Eepersip in one flaming mass, kissing her with their feathery wings. Making her way over to the pool, she saw her reflection, a shimmer of gold.

A light darted out toward her from the woods; then another and yet another, until there were hundreds of lights flickering and blinking at her from all corners of the great field – the lights of elves and gnomes, little fairies of the field. And she danced happily among them – danced until the dawn appeared on the horizon, sending away the darkness and making the stars fade into space. It flushed the whole sky with rose, sent arms of it even as far as the west; arms and streamers of color which paled toward their tips. Little white clouds grew pink, too, and the color was reflected on the distant mountaintops. Again the snow-field seemed to become fire – fire which was soon quenched by the coolness of the snow. As the sun sent its first golden beams above the horizon, the color faded, turned to yellow, and soon entirely disappeared. Then the sky was blue-deep, quivering blue, with the fluffy clouds like pearls in an azure setting.

Suddenly Eepersip saw that she was dressed in a flouncy array of spring crocuses and maidenhair ferns. Lovely flowers of pink and yellow were entwined in her hair, and butterflies fluttered around her. She danced happily and leaped high in the air. How free and light she felt in the lovely dress that had been given her!

That day Eepersip was even happier than usual. She floated about, visiting each flower, each bush and tree. She played games with the butterflies, the games she had played on the old meadow, that first summer of her life in the House without Windows. When she rested, she sat on top of a laurel-bush, and not a twig bent beneath her. The slightest breeze blew her about, changed the direction of her dance. Butterfly after butterfly flew to her, flock after flock, as if they had some message to tell her; and after each visit she was happier than before. Yes, they were messengers, these happy creatures; messengers who came to whisper her a secret – a secret from Nature, a secret of the beautiful meadow, a secret from the fairies.

And, when the sun again tinged the sky with color, a flock of these butterflies, of purple and gold and green, came swooping and alighted on her head in a circle, the largest in front. Others came in myriads and covered her dress with delicate wing-touches. Eepersip held out her arms a moment: A gold- and-black one alighted on each wrist. And then – she rose into the air, and, hovering an instant over a great laurel-bush, vanished.

She was a fairy – a wood-nymph. She would be invisible forever to all mortals, save those few who have minds to believe, eyes to see. To these she is ever present, the spirit of Nature – a sprite of the meadow, a naiad of lakes, a nymph of the woods.

CHAPTER IV
HISTORICAL NOTE
(By Another Hand)

IN THE OPENING WEEK of January, 1923, there appeared on the outside of a certain door within a dingy, sunless, and cramped apartment a slip of paper bearing the following typewritten notice:

```
Nobody may come into this room
if the door is shut tight (if
it is shut not quite latched it
is all right) without knocking.
The person in the room if he
agrees that one shall come in
will say "come in,"or some-
thing like that and if he does
not agree to it he will say "Not
yet, please,"or something like
that. The door may be shut if
nobody is in the room but if a
person wants to come in, knocks
and hears no answer that means
that there is no one in the room
and he must not go in.

Reason. If the door is shut
tight and a person is in the
room the shut door means that
the person in the room wishes to
be left alone.
```

The author of this odd manifesto (here reproduced with strict textual exactitude from the frayed original) was the author of the foregoing story, then just three months short of nine years old. The door on which it appeared was that of the room in which, on a small typewriter, she wrote down the adventures of Eepersip, and the week in which it appeared was that in which these adventures had their beginning.

She finished them, in the same room, three months later, early in the March of her ninth completed year and a few days after her birthday. One of her curious, slightly un-American inventions, I must here explain, was the concept of her own birthday as an annual occasion for handing out things to the other members of her family. She planned this story from the beginning as a gift for her mother on March 4. Would her mother "like" it, though? On that point there would have to be a disinterested opinion as it happened, mine. With intense secrecy, behind the latched door of that room guarded by the constrained preparatory notice, she read me the instalments as they were produced.

My candid guess was that her mother would indeed "like" it. I liked it myself, if only as unconscious expression of a radiant physical vitality – so much I found in it of the mighty swimmer, the enjoyable young comrade of trail and river, always ready to swing a paddle tirelessly or carry un- grumbling a full fair share of pack. I "liked" it, too, as her answer to the one year which she had ever been called upon to spend in undeniably tawdry surroundings.

But, alas, there came interruptions – one of them in the shape of the only appreciable illness she has ever had – and these pulled down her average daily output. On her big days the small typist clicked off fresh copy to the extent of from four to five thousand words; but still the appointed morning caught her, some pages short of the end. The tale came to Finis a few days later. Its length, in that first incarnation, was some 40,000 words, or not far from what it is now.

Up to that point there had been, of course, no thought of print. It was I who introduced the question of print; and it had at that time no connection whatever with publication. The author of the story never had (and never has) experienced any school system, public or private, her education having been exclusively the home-made one devised by her mother; and I was beginning to think it high time that print became a part of it. It was, in fine, my idea that we ought to have a piece of her work put into type in some small shop where she could set part of it herself, pull her own proofs, learn more about proof- reading by correcting them, and see the whole thing through to the binding of a small armful of copies for her friends.

But before anything of that sort was done I wanted her to have the practice of revising her first copy as carefully as possible and putting it into strictly printable condition – as, indeed, she was eager to do. Accordingly she took it away with her in the summer, worked on it from early July through September in the intervals of swimming, canoeing, mountain-climbing, and plain day-dreaming, and brought it back, on the 5th of October, 1923, ready for print. Twenty-four hours later we left it in a burning building from which nothing got out but the lucky human occupants.

*****

From the point of view of an admittedly fond parent – for I can make no slightest pretension to the ability to contemplate all this with a stranger's or a critic's detachment – it was heart-rending to watch the nine-year-old author torture her memory to the end of reconstituting the tale in its first shape. There were, during the next weeks, a good many blank hours at the typewriter, and it was slowly and painfully that page followed page. At this rate, it was going to take about three years merely to salvage what had once been manufactured out of the void in three months.

Then, one day in December, everything was suddenly different. As an experiment of despair, Barbara had stopped trying to remember the shape of sentences, the precise order and phraseology of details, and had begun to let the material come back as it listed. And to her astonishment it came in a freshet, like northern rivers when the ice goes out. When, a few days later, we put work aside to organize our makeshift Christmas, she was still in a happy glow, the first third of the fantasy existed again, and the story was running over its banks.

There followed one interruption after another, and it was not until the autumn of 1924 that the second draft was completed. In the late winter of 1924-25, Barbara worked patiently through the first third, putting it in what she hoped would be final shape. The manuscript had to be laid away in May of 1925, and was not touched again far nine months. Then, in February and March, 1926, she did her revision of the second and third parts, made a few minor improvements in Part I, and typed out a fair copy of the whole – the copy from which this little book is set.

To what extent is this twelve-year-old manuscript identical with the nine-year-old story? To a far greater extent, I am sure, than seems compatible with the huge number of hours spent on it since it was completed; for it happens that a disproportionate number of those hours has gone into laborious, at times unconscious, recovery of the precise effects which were in the last original. The differences are not where a stranger to the author would naturally look for them: that is, in the diction and the build of sentences.

Barbara's vocabulary at nine was, of course, a stratified arrangement of deposits from Walter de la Mare and George Macdonald, W. H. Hudson[1] and Mark Twain, Shelley and Scott; that is to say, it was just what it is now except for the later addition of words which could not be in this story anyhow – the words of history, of science.

And certainly the fundamental ideas and emotions of the story have undergone no change. The fact is, it was conceived and written at the end of a phase which could not return – that phase of normal childhood in which nature means nearly everything and civilization nearly nothing. The whole purport of Eepersip's existence is simply a healthy nine-year-old consciousness made articulate – something that an eleven-year-old could recover only by a feat of the memory, and an adult mind only by an improbable *tour de force* of the imagination. Barbara, in short, designed this curious narrative at the last moment when to do so would have been at all open to her. By no human possibility could it have been in her head at eleven if she had not had it down on paper at nine.

The chief differences, then, between the printed and the destroyed versions represent the inevitable development of the author's taste in minor particulars, and they are these: (1) There is appreciably less of the pursuit-and-escape device, and correspondingly more of the sheer reveling in natural beauty; (2) a great many exact measurements, in the form of dates, distances, rates, heights, and depths, have been omitted as realistic and therefore trivializing; (3) there is a somewhat maturer attempt to keep the fauna and flora consistent with latitude, altitude, and season; and (4) the lapse of time is managed rather more consciously and coherently than it was in the first place. If, in the treatment of these and other details of the story, there seems to be a progressive increase in maturity, that is a consequence and a measure of the nine months' interval between the author's revision of Part I and her revision of Parts II and III.

It will be observed that the differences involve little or no addition. The one piece of addition is in the episode of Eepersip's young sister Fleuriss, which is considerably more developed. The obvious reason for this is that the author's own young sister, at the time of the first draft, existed only as an insistent demand on Barbara's part; whereas in the period of the revision she was a dream fulfilled, subject to adoring daily observation.

As to ordinary literacy, there is no perceptible difference, and has been none since the typewritten by-products of Barbara's sixth and seventh years. In short, what the reader is here given is an articulate eight- and nine-year-old child's outpouring of her own dreams and longings in a fanciful tale, superficially revised by the hand of a twelve-year-old girl whose life on its more artificial side is made up principally of books and music.

*****

It was the youthful author's idea, not mine, that her story should be accompanied by a word of explanation from her father. I do not know how, when, or exactly why she formulated such a requirement, any more than I can explain where she got many another of the ideas with which she has been known to startle or confound me. Long after the story had been completed and while it was undergoing revision, there arrived a day on which I was told that the requirement existed; that Barbara had secretly been counting on me, and with pleasure in the thought. Pleasure! If I could give that, and so easily, and to her, it was not mine to make a gesture of resistance. I insist only that what I have to say shall be placed where it can stand between no reader and the story.

It would be neither good manners nor good sense for me to attempt any sort of appraisal of this chronicle, of Eepersip's adventures in the spacious rooms of her House without Windows. I have been too near to the whole thing, and am too near the chronicler. The most that I can now add without impropriety is a statement of why the first thought, a book to be manufactured but by no means published, gave way after all to a different idea.

It began to strike me that here was something representatively valuable – valuable, I mean, as a representation of something lovely in generalized childhood itself – and yet not so very likely to achieve frequent expression. The fact is that the impulses crystallized in this story mostly fade into the light of common day a year or two before the dawn of that amount of mechanical articulacy which is necessary for a tangible expression of them; and they are therefore almost never expressed. Actually, I do not happen to be acquainted with a single prose document of much scope which achieves the full expression, or any first-hand expression, of what is in a normal healthy child's mind and heart during that mysterious phase when butterflies, flowers, winging swallows, and white-capped waves are twice as real as even a quite bearable parent, and incomparably more important – the phase before there is any unshakable Tyranny of Things.

What is probably unusual about Barbara is the conspiracy of the circumstances which have made these two things, the phase and the necessary articulacy, overlap. She is not precocious, and the phase may have lasted a year or two longer than it does in many. She is not excessively gregarious and has not been regimented in schools and groups: therefore nothing has as yet standardized her, or ironed out her spontaneity, or made her particularly ashamed of it. She has been given plenty of time to know herself.

And, almost above all, having used a typewriter as a plaything from a time that she can't remember, she was able to rattle off an easy 1200 words an hour, without any awareness of the physical process, years before penmanship could have developed half the proficiency, even with intense concentration on the physical process alone.

I formed, then, the opinion that her Eepersip, who lives an ardent life of three or four years in nearly every child's unconsciousness, lives not at all anywhere in the world's multitude of books. And it came to seem to me that this Eepersip very possibly has something to say to you about your children, and about yourself of a time that you may easily have forgotten, as well as, perhaps, to your children directly.

A last point: Barbara has been given by her parents, in the final preparation of this manuscript, exactly what help she has asked for. That is not nearly so much help as many an adult author often has from us, for there is not one idea or structural change of ours in the entire story. But I see no value in withholding solicited advice in order to make a Roman holiday for those who like to chuckle or guffaw over infantile slips in spelling and grammar. Barbara, whose spelling and grammar happen to be very reliable, would want us to straighten them out for her if they weren't; and we should do it. When she asks whether a comma will do or ought it to be a semi-colon? we answer as well as we can. When she wants to know: "Have I made it clear what this means?" or "Have I used this word twice too near together?" of course we say how it strikes us. Annoyingly from my Yankee point of view, she insists on a preference for Oxford spelling, undoubtedly met in three out of four of the contemporary books which she reads.

Well, then, I point out to her that if she is going to spell "color" she must also spell "favorite" and "story" and "veranda." But the words themselves, the sentences, are hers, just as truly as is the pattern of the whole; and hers is a really workmanlike care for weeding out gawky constructions and repetitions of the words of which she has been successively over-fond.

One of the great objects of imaginative writing, I take it, is to have joy. Another, not wholly separable from the first, is to learn as you go. I like to suppose that Barbara, just turned twelve, is having her just share of both.

WILSON FOLLETT

March 1926

ABOUT THE AUTHOR

Barbara Newhall Follett was born March 4th, 1914 in Hanover, New Hampshire and disappeared December 1939 in Brookline, Massachusetts. Barbara Newhall Follett's father was Wilson Follett, an English teacher at Dartmouth College, who became a well-known editor and writer of the book, *Follett's Modern American Usage*. Her mother was Helen Thomas Follett, a writer in her own right who later in life published two travel books.

A turning point for Barbara was her fascination with her father's typewriter. "Tell me a story about it," she demanded, and after her father explained how it worked, she began furiously producing her thoughts onto paper.

When she was four years old, she met an elderly Swedish gentleman who restored antiques, Mr. Oberg. Her stuffed toy rabbit had lost an eye, and Mr. Oberg paused in his work on two ancient clocks to repair her rabbit. Barbara was so impressed that not long afterward she composed her first important correspondence, a story in Mr. Oberg's honor, and signed it with her full name:

Twelve clocks were on a shelf all ticking away.

They wanted to take a walk, so they Jumped down and started.
A little dog saw them and pushed one over, then another, and finally all.
They were broken into pieces. Then Mr. Oberg came along and said:
"Oh my!" and put the pieces into a basket and took them home.
He mended them; and now they are as good as new.

Barbara Newhall Follett

Believing Barbara would receive a better education at home rather than public or private school, the Follett's decided to design their own homeschool curriculum for Barbara, primarily created by Helen Follett.

When she was five years old, she was writing quite long stories, including a tale called *The Life of the Spinning Wheel, the Rocking-Horse, and the Rabbit,* which was unusually imaginative with a full- bodied vocabulary. The story is reproduced in the book, *Barbara, the Unconscious Biography of a Child Genius,* a much later book published in 1966 based on Barbara's letters and stories.

In 1922, at age seven, Barbara, who played the violin, was composing striking poetry based on her music:

When I go to orchestra rehearsals,
there are often several passages for the Triangle and Tambourine
together.
When they are together,
they sound like a big piece of metal that has broken in thousandths
and is falling to the ground.

When she was eight years old, she began work on *The House Without Windows* as a gift for her mother. After the first manuscript was destroyed in a fire, it was recreated over a period of a few years, finally completed when she was eleven, and published in 1927 when she was twelve to great acclaim.

After publication of her novel, Barbara became fascinated with the sea and convinced her parents the next summer to allow her to accompany the crew of a ship, the Frederick H., a three-masted schooner bound for Nova Scotia. Though she was supposed to be a passenger, she insisted on doing chores as a deck-hand. After returning home, she turned her adventure into a novel, *The Voyage of the Norman D.,* which was accepted for publication in 1928 when she was thirteen years old. Barbara was famous.

During this time, her father was spending more and more time in New York, and shortly after her latest novel was published, she received the news that her father was leaving the family for another woman. This devastated Barbara, who was very close to her father.

During the next few years, she and her mother travelled to several countries with Helen hoping to publish a travelogue of their adventures. This was not immediately successful, and they were forced to return to the United States. Barbara for some time was left with friends in Los Angeles, a place she "loathed," particularly when she began attending school. She ran away to San Francisco, but was reported as a runaway, and was picked up by authorities. The case made national headlines.

All of this was especially tragic timing, as 1929 brought the beginning of the Great Depression and after returning and being reunited in New York, Helen Follett and Barbara found themselves very tight for money. Barbara was forced at age sixteen to get a job in New York as a typist after taking a course in shorthand and business typing, "a decidedly more tawdry use of its magic," as she described it.

In June, she wrote to a friend, "*My dreams are going through their death flurries, I thought they were all safely buried, but sometimes they stir in their grave, making my heartstrings twinge. I mean no particular dream, you understand, but the whole radiant flock of them together—with their rainbow wings, iridescent, bright, soaring, glorious, sublime. They are dying before the steel javelins and arrows of a world of Time and Money.*"

By 1934, she had written two more books, *Lost Island,* a novel, and *Travels Without a Donkey,* a travelogue. But they were never published.

Around this time, she met a man named Nickerson Rogers, an outdoorsman who shared her love of nature. They soon eloped and had adventures backpacking through Europe. They settled down in Brookline, Massachusetts where they were relatively secure and happy, at least for some time. Barbara took dance classes during the summers at Mills College, which she loved.

In 1939, she believed Rogers was seeing another woman. She wrote to a friend, "*There is someone else… I had it coming to me, I know.*"

Later in the same letter, she wrote, "*I think I've persuaded him to give me my chance. He is a very kind person, really, and hates to hurt people. He hated to write that letter; that's why it sounded so awful. I think that, if I can really prove that I'm different, why maybe things will work out. He still doesn't quite believe it, as he says, that a leopard can change its spots! He thinks that in a month things will be all wrong again. So I say, at least let me have that month! I think I'll get it, and I think I can win if I've got the strength."*

A later letter showed that Barbara was hopeful things could be salvaged: "*I had had the feeling up till then that he definitely did not want to [make a go of things]. So imagine my amazement, my almost hysterical delight, when he said yes, he wanted to make a go of it."*

But the good feelings were not to last: "*I don't know what to say now. On the surface, things are terribly, terribly calm, and wrong – just as wrong as they can be. I am trying – we both are trying. I still think there is a chance that the outcome will be a happy one; but I would have to think that anyway in order to live; so you can draw any conclusions you like from that!"*

That was Barbara's last letter to her friend, or to anyone else as far as is known. On Thursday, December 7, 1939, Barbara and Nick quarreled, and she left their Brookline apartment that evening with $30 and a notebook.

She was never heard from again.

Nick, after she didn't return, reported her missing two weeks later. The bureau of Missing Persons sent out a five-state alarm, but to no avail. Some believed she had run away, perhaps to her friend in California, but no evidence or communication from her has ever surfaced.

Barbara Newhall Follett, brilliant and once famous, simply disappeared and was never seen again. All that is left is her brilliant writing that she accomplished at such a young and tender age.

OTHER TITLES BY 'LIL BEETHOVEN PUBLISHERS

Diamond as Big as the Ritz by F. Scott Fitzgerald
The Romance Of Lust, or Early Experiences, Uncensored; A classic Victorian erotic novel by Anonymous
Mrs. Dalloway by Virginia Woolf
Torchlight Parade by Jéanpaul Ferro
The Great Gatsby by F. Scott Fitzgerald
Suicide Six by Anonymous
Frankenstein by Mary Shelley
The Scarlet Letter by Nathaniel Hawthorne
Narrative of the Life of Frederick Douglass by Frederick Douglass
Dracula by Bram Stoker
The Bloody Tenant of Persecution by Roger Williams
The General History of Virginia, New England, & the Summer Isles, 1624 by John Smith;
Of Plymouth Plantation, 1620 in Modern English by William Bradford
Of Plymouth Plantation, 1620 in Old English by William Bradford
Algonquian, A Key into the Native Language of America, 1643 by Roger Williams
The Souls of Black Folk by W.E.B Du Bois
The Shunned House by H.P. Lovecraft

Printed in Great Britain
by Amazon

32264836R00051